SHARKEY'S RAIDERS

On his release from jail, veteran bank robber J. C. Sharkey plans one last bank raid, the big one that will make him rich. He recruits what he considers to be the perfect gang for the job. However, Pinkerton detective Phineas Yeats is hot on the trail of one of his gang and two of the others are responsible for the massacre of a caravan of Mexican traders. Adding to Sharkey's troubles are the untimely interventions of seductive saloon singer Arizona Audrey and the famous Kentuckian gunfighter Jack Stone . . .

Books by J. D. Kincaid
in the Linford Western Library:

CORRIGAN'S REVENGE
THE FOURTH OF JULY
SHOWDOWN AT MEDICINE CREEK
COYOTE WINTER
JUDGEMENT AT RED ROCK
THE MAN WHO TAMED MALLORY
GHOST TOWN
THE LEGEND OF INJUN JOE BRADY
INCIDENT AT MUSTANG PASS

SPECIAL MESSAGE TO READERS

This book is published under the auspices of

THE ULVERSCROFT FOUNDATION

(registered charity No. 264873 UK)

Established in 1972 to provide funds for research, diagnosis and treatment of eye diseases. Examples of contributions made are: —

A Children's Assessment Unit at Moorfield's Hospital, London.

•

Twin operating theatres at the Western Ophthalmic Hospital, London.

•

A Chair of Ophthalmology at the Royal Australian College of Ophthalmologists.

•

The Ulverscroft Children's Eye Unit at the Great Ormond Street Hospital For Sick Children, London.

You can help further the work of the Foundation by making a donation or leaving a legacy. Every contribution, no matter how small, is received with gratitude. Please write for details to:

THE ULVERSCROFT FOUNDATION,
The Green, Bradgate Road, Anstey,
Leicester LE7 7FU, England.
Telephone: (0116) 236 4325

In Australia write to:
THE ULVERSCROFT FOUNDATION,
c/o The Royal Australian and New Zealand
College of Ophthalmologists,
94-98 Chalmers Street, Surry Hills,
N.S.W. 2010, Australia

J. D. KINCAID

SHARKEY'S RAIDERS

Complete and Unabridged

LINFORD
Leicester

First published in Great Britain in 2004 by
Robert Hale Limited
London

First Linford Edition
published 2005
by arrangement with
Robert Hale Limited
London

British Library CIP Data

Kincaid, J. D.
Sharkey's raiders.—Large print ed.—
Linford western library
1. Western stories
2. Large type books
I. Title
823.9′14 [F]

ISBN 1–84395–772–8

Published by
F. A. Thorpe (Publishing)
Anstey, Leicestershire

Set by Words & Graphics Ltd.
Anstey, Leicestershire
Printed and bound in Great Britain by
T. J. International Ltd., Padstow, Cornwall

This book is printed on acid-free paper

1

Phineas Yeats removed his grey Derby and mopped his brow. He was riding south through the Nevada desert in the year of Our Lord 1883 and, although it was mid-October, the temperature remained in the high nineties.

Yeats replaced his hat and rode on. Taking a route through the sagebrush roughly parallel to the Old Spanish Trail, he entered the Las Vegas Valley. Ahead of him, he spotted a lone rider wending his way through the foothills of the Sheep Range mountains. Yeats smiled grimly.

Phineas Yeats was a Pinkerton man, at present employed by that Detective Agency to track down and capture the outlaw, Sam McCluskey. A month earlier, in a botched stagecoach hold-up, McCluskey had shot and wounded both the driver and the guard and killed one of the passengers. Unfortunately for McCluskey, the passenger happened to be a vice-president of the Kansas Pacific Railway Company. In consequence, the company had engaged the services of the Pinkerton Detective Agency to bring the outlaw to justice.

Sam McCluskey was a big man and, at the time of the attempted hold-up, had been wearing a black Stetson, a knee-length buckskin jacket and denim pants and riding a bay horse. Yeats had struck lucky in Cherry Creek. According to the town marshal, a stranger answering to that description had ridden through the previous day, heading south. Yeats had figured the outlaw would steer clear of the recognized trails, and, assuming the lone rider was in fact McCluskey, it seemed he had guessed right.

Yeats continued to gain on his quarry. He did not, however, quicken his pace, for he had no wish to alarm the horseman. He did not know how his pinto would match the other's bay for speed or stamina, and, having found him so easily, he didn't want to lose him.

The distance between the two riders steadily decreased. Yeats' smile widened. He pushed back the jacket of his grey, three-piece, city-style suit and dropped his right hand on to the butt of his Remington revolver. Presently, he rode abreast of the stranger and, pulling the gun from its holster, aimed it at the big man and yelled, 'OK, pull up an' keep your hands where I can see 'em!'

The big man did as he was bid, then turned to face the Pinkerton agent.

'I ain't worth robbin',' he said quietly.

Phineas Yeats studied the big man closely. He fitted the description Yeats had of Sam McCluskey almost exactly: tall, wide-shouldered, with grey-flecked brown hair and a rugged, square-cut face, and wearing a grey Stetson, a grey shirt beneath a knee-length buckskin jacket and denim pants. No mention had been made of the red kerchief round the man's thick, strong neck and the colour of the Stetson had been given as black rather than grey. But, then, a man might easily change his hat and, as for the kerchief . . .

Yeats felt confident he had his man. He smiled coldly and said, 'I ain't no road agent.'

'No?' said the big man.

'Nope. Name's Phineas Yeats an' I represent the Pinkerton Detective Agency.'

'So, why are you pointin' that gun at me? I ain't no concern of your goddam detective agency.'

'Oh, but you are!'

'In what way?'

'I'm arrestin' you for the murder of Hiram P. Netherton an' I'm takin' you back north to Carson City to stand trial.'

'You got the wrong man, Mr Yeats.'

'I don't think so.'

'Wa'al, who in tarnation d'you reckon I am?'

'I don't reckon. I know. You're the outlaw, Sam McCluskey.'

The big man laughed. 'Call yourself a detective?' he sneered.

'I *am* a detective,' retorted Yeats.

'A pretty darned useless one if'n you figure I'm McCluskey. He's a two-bit hold-up artist who, I'll concede, bears some kinda passin' resemblance to me, but — '

'His description fits you exactly.'

'Not exactly, 'cause I ain't him.'

'Says you.'

'Yeah, says me. An', Mr Yeats, I don't take too kindly to your pointin' that there gun at me.'

'That's a shame.'

'Sure is,' said the big man, and he promptly began to swing himself out of the saddle.

'Hey, what in blue blazes d'you think you're doin'?' demanded Phineas Yeats.

'Jest dismountin', Mr Yeats.'

'No! Hold on! Hey . . . '

The Pinkerton detective had been half-expecting his quarry to go for his gun. He had not expected him to simply dismount. This threw him. He hesitated and, in that split second, the man vanished behind his bay gelding. A moment later, he re-appeared, diving beneath the horse's belly and coming up clutching a Frontier Model Colt. Yeats redirected the Remington, but he was too late. Before he could squeeze the trigger, the Frontier Model Colt belched fire and a .45 calibre slug thudded into his right shoulder and blasted him clean out of the saddle.

Phineas Yeats hit the ground with a tremendous thump. The wind was knocked out of him and then, as the dust settled and he recovered his senses, he looked round wildly for his revolver, which had been jerked from his grasp. It lay on the desert floor, a good ten yards away. He glanced upwards into the muzzle of the big man's Colt.

The big man viewed Yeats with a wry grin. He noted the detective's thin, pale face, his sad brown eyes and drooping black moustache, his jet black hair, lily-white hands and slim build. The

Pinkerton man was evidently a townsman.

For his part, Phineas Yeats gazed up into the big man's faded blue eyes and gasped, 'OK, so why don't you just kill me an' git it over with?'

'An' why would I wanta do that?' asked the other.

''Cause you're a goddam murderin' sonofabitch who — '

'Sam McCluskey's a goddam murderin' sonofabitch.'

'Yeah.'

'I told you, I ain't Sam McCluskey.'

'Then, who the hell are you?'

'The name's Stone — Jack Stone.'

There was a short silence. Finally, Yeats spoke. His voice was low. He spoke almost in a whisper.

'Jack Stone. You're Jack Stone?'

'Yup.'

While Yeats was Chicago born and bred and most of his investigations on behalf of the Pinkerton Detective Agency had been conducted in the various West Coast cities, he had once worked on a case in Dodge City. Consequently, he had heard of Jack Stone, the Kentuckian who had helped Bat Masterson clean up that town and who had later become a legend of the West as the man who tamed Mallory, the roughest, toughest town in Colorado.

'You still a lawman, Mr Stone?' he enquired.

'Nope,' said Stone.

'Ah!'

'Figured I'd retire an' enjoy the quiet life.'

'So, what you doin' these days?'

'Aw, this an' that! Jest finished drivin' a herd of Texas longhorns up from San Antonio to the cattle-yards at Los Angeles.'

'An' you call that the quiet life!'

'It's a heap better'n forever layin' my life on the line as a peace officer.'

'I guess so.' Yeats continued to stare up at the Kentuckian. He muttered reproachfully, 'Did you have to go an' shoot me? I'd've thought that, as a one-time peace officer . . . '

'Anyone points a gun at me, be he a Pinkerton man, US marshal, sheriff or whoever, he's liable to git hisself shot,' retorted Stone.

'But, if'n you'd let me take you back to Carson City . . . '

'The good folks there might easily have taken your word for it that I was Sam McCluskey.'

'I don't think so. I'm sure the truth would have come out an' you'd've walked free.'

'Mebbe. But I had no wish to ride all the way to Carson City to find out.'

'No, I s'pose not.'

'Anyways, what convinced you, Mr Yeats, that I was McCluskey?'

'Wa'al, he'd been spotted ridin' south outa Cherry Creek an' his general description fitted you. The clincher was, he was wearin' a knee-length buckskin jacket. You'll allow buckskin jackets ain't that common.'

'No, they ain't. Didn't it occur to you, though, that, bein' as he was on the run, McCluskey would've had the sense to ditch that there jacket an' buy hisself another, less conspicuous one?'

'You're right, Mr Stone; I should've thought of that,' conceded Phineas Yeats.

'Wa'al, you sure paid for your mistake,' said Stone. 'Let's take a look at your wound.'

He crouched down beside the injured Pinkerton agent and carefully, gently, helped him up into a sitting position. Then he proceeded to remove Yeats' jacket, vest and shirt. This done, he examined the wound, wiping away the blood with the tail of Yeats' shirt.

'The good news is, the bullet's gone straight through. The bad news is, you've lost one helluva lot of blood,' he announced.

'Yeah. I sure don't feel too good,' confessed Yeats.

'The Las Vegas Ranch is only a coupla miles further on,' said Stone. 'I'll fix you up as best I can, an' then, if you can ride that far, I'm sure there'll be someone there to patch you up properly. OK, Mr Yeats?'

'OK. Oh, an' you'd best call me Phineas. Considerin' you shot me, there ain't no reason to be so goddam formal!'

Stone grinned.

'Fine. You call me Jack.'

The Kentuckian tore Yeats' shirt into pieces and used these to plug and bind the wound, thereby decreasing, if not entirely halting, further loss of blood. Then, he helped the detective to his feet, aided him to don his vest and jacket and handed him his Derby hat.

'Now all I gotta do is git back into the saddle,' said a white-faced Phineas Yeats.

'You can do it,' Stone assured him.

'I guess so,' said Yeats doubtfully.

'Sure you can.'

Stone was right. With a great deal of help from him, the Pinkerton man eventually succeeded in clambering back into the saddle. He took hold of the reins and set the pinto off at a slow trot. Stone rode alongside, ready to steady the other should the necessity arise.

The two men cut through the sagebrush and between the mesquite, yucca and Joshua trees that dotted the desert, to join the Old Spanish Trail. This led straight to the Las Vegas Ranch, an oasis in the midst of the dreary desert, where water was abundant and, consequently, a resting place for those travelling both north and south along the trail.

When presently they reached the ranch, it was dusk and they found they were not the only travellers to have halted there. A small Mexican caravan travelling northwards from Santa Fe was already in the process of setting up camp. The caravan was led by one Pedro Fernandez and was transporting hand-woven blankets to Los Angeles, something the Mexicans did in the fall of every year.

Stone had intended seeking help

from the ranch-house, which lay half-a-mile from the spot where the Mexicans were camped. However, he was waylaid by Fernandez, whose keen eye had quickly spotted that Stone's companion was in imminent danger of falling from the saddle.

'I see your friend is wounded, *señor*,' he said.

'Yes.'

'Can I help?'

'Thanks. If'n you'd give me a hand to git him down off his hoss?' said Stone.

'But, of course, *señor*,' he said.

Between them, the Mexican and the Kentuckian lifted Phineas Yeats from his saddle and gently laid him down on the ground. Thereupon, Fernandez called upon his wife to tend to the wounded man.

She quickly set to the task while Stone, Fernandez and the rest of the Mexicans stood round and watched.

When she had finished, she rose and spoke quietly in Spanish to her husband. He turned to the Kentuckian.

'Maria, she says she has done what she can, but it is best your *amigo* should see a doctor.'

'Yeah. Wa'al, thanks, ma'am.' Stone raised his hat to Maria before asking Fernandez, 'Have you any idea whereabouts I'm likely to find a doctor?'

Fernandez shrugged his shoulders.

'I do not know, *señor*, but perhaps Señor Stewart can tell you?'

Stone nodded. He had passed through the Las Vegas Valley before and knew that the ranch, which bordered the campsite used by travellers of the Old Spanish Trail, was owned by a Scot named Archibald Stewart.

'I'll mosey on over an' ask him,' said Stone.

'And we will take care of your *amigo*,' stated Fernandez. 'When you return, you must both share our supper.'

'Thanks, Mr er . . . ?'

'Fernandez.'

'Thanks, Mr Fernandez. My name's

Stone an' my friend's is Yeats.'

'I see. And how was Señor Yeats shot? Was it perhaps bandits who — '

'An accident. It was an accident,' said Phineas Yeats from his reclining position beside the campfire.

'That's right,' agreed Stone, whereupon he remounted his bay gelding and cantered off towards the ranch-house.

Upon his return a few minutes later, he joined Yeats and the Mexicans round the campfire. They enjoyed an excellent meal of enchiladas crammed with goat's cheese, tomatoes and peppers and soaked in chilli sauce, washed down with rich, black coffee. And, while they ate, Stone told the others what he had learned from Archibald Stewart.

'There's a small silver-minin' town 'bout seven miles north-west of here, name of Bonnie Springs. There's a doctor there who Mr Stewart reckons is pretty darned good,' he said.

'I don't care how pretty darned good

he is,' declared Yeats. 'I ain't seein' him tonight, for I'm plumb tuckered out.'

'Bonnie Springs is not on the Old Spanish Trail,' said Fernandez.

'Nope. I realize that,' drawled Stone.

'Señor Yeats will not reach town unaided,' said the Mexican.

'I'll be fine in the mornin'. Gimme a good night's rest an' I'll easily ride those seven miles,' remarked Yeats.

'But you have lost too much blood, *señor!*'

'No, I . . . '

'It's OK,' interjected Stone. 'I'll ride with Señor Yeats an' make sure he gits there.'

'But you were headin' south, Jack. I cain't ask you to turn about an' — '

'I ain't goin' nowhere in a hurry, while Señor Fernandez an' his folks are aimin' north to Los Angeles, where they got goods to sell. Am I right?'

'That is correct, *señor*,' said Fernandez.

'So, you see, Phineas, if'n you want company — an' you sure as hell *need* company if you're to make it to Bonnie

Springs — then you're stuck with me,' stated the Kentuckian.

Phineas Yeats smiled weakly.

'So be it,' he said, and, rolling over, fell instantly asleep.

2

Despite the early-morning coolness, Jack Stone reckoned they could expect another hot day. It was crucial, therefore, that he and the Pinkerton man set forth for Bonnie Springs as soon as possible. Phineas Yeats, in his present weakened state, was unlikely to manage the seven-mile ride in the full heat of the sun.

They joined Pedro Fernandez and the rest of the Mexicans in a simple breakfast of soft tacos, washed down with the same rich, black coffee they had drunk on the previous evening.

Finally, it was time to go.

'Wa'al, thanks for everythin',' said Yeats, grasping Fernandez with his left hand. His right arm remained in the sling Maria had prepared for him.

'I hope that you will reach Bonnie

Springs OK, *señor*,' replied the Mexican.

'I'll see he gits there,' promised Stone.

'Of course.'

'You take care of yourself now,' declared the Kentuckian.

'I will, *señor*.' Fernandez grinned. Then, having helped Yeats mount, he raised his sombrero and cried, '*Adios amigos*!'

''Bye. An' good luck!' said Yeats.

'Yeah. Have a safe ride,' added Stone.

The two riders cut across the desert towards the nearby mountains, heading for the silver-mining town of Bonnie Springs which nestled at their base. Fernandez watched them go, before turning and instructing his fellow Mexicans to break camp. He was anxious to get underway as they had several hundred miles still to cover before they reached Los Angeles.

The caravan consisted of Pedro Fernandez and his wife and eight others — six men and two women. The men rode on small black horses, the women on ponies, and they led half-a-dozen mules bearing heavy loads of colourful, handwoven blankets. This was the sixth caravan headed by Fernandez since taking over as leader from his father. A small, stocky man, he rode proudly ahead, setting the pace for the caravan as it proceeded northwards along the Old Spanish Trail.

Morning passed into afternoon. The sun beat down unmercifully as the caravan followed the trail, which snaked through the sagebrush, skirting the foothills of the Sheep Range mountains. The desert stretched ahead, vast and desolate, in stark contrast to the Las Vegas basin with its cottonwoods and willow-shaded grass. Knowing that it would be several days before they reached the next springs, Fernandez was grateful for the supplies of water, which they had picked up at Las Vegas. He lit a cheroot and, smoking contentedly, continued to ride ahead, his eyes fixed on the distant horizon.

It was mid-afternoon when Luis Delgado spotted the caravan from his hill-top vantage point. He glanced at his brother José and smiled. The thin, cruel smile flickered swiftly across his lips and was gone. His eyes narrowed beneath the wide brim of his sombrero. He knew what he and José must do.

The two brothers, although born only a year apart, were quite dissimilar. Luis Delgado was tall and lanky, with a hawkish visage and a long, drooping moustache. He took after his father, while José had his mother's characteristics: a short, stocky frame and a round, moon-shaped face. He boasted neither whiskers nor beard. Both wore sombreros and vari-coloured ponchos. Beneath the ponchos they each packed a pair of Remington revolvers, while each of their saddle-boots held a Winchester. In addition, Luis Delgado carried a Bowie knife in a sheath on his belt. To say they were armed to the teeth would be no exaggeration. But, then, the two brothers were bandits, wanted both in

Mexico and in various states across the Union.

Theirs was a fearsome reputation, although they had in fact been relatively unsuccessful in their chosen profession, the many robberies they conducted having gained them very little. It was not the sums of money they had taken that earned them their notoriety. It was their sheer ferocity and utter ruthlessness that made the Delgado brothers feared in every state they had visited. Not content with simply robbing their victims, they invariably murdered and, in the case of women, raped them. Neither Luis nor José Delgado ever showed one ounce of compassion or pity.

'We meet Señor McCluskey at Bonnie Springs,' said Luis Delgado.

'Yes,' said his brother.

'It is only a few miles from here.'

'Yes.'

'And it will surely have a peace officer, either a sheriff or a town marshal.'

'Yes.'

'Who will hold a list of Wanted notices.'

'Yes.'

'So, we shall need a disguise.'

'Yes. But where do we get such a thing?'

Luis Delgado pointed to the caravan proceeding sedately northwards along the Old Spanish Trail.

'We disguise ourselves as traders,' he said quietly.

José chuckled.

'Our fellow countrymen are most obliging. They appear just when we need them,' he said.

'That is so, my brother,' grinned Luis Delgado.

'We kill all of them?'

'Of course.'

The two brothers urged their horses forward. They cantered down out of the foothills and across the desert, aiming to intercept the caravan as it continued to press northwards along the trail.

Presently, they emerged out of the sagebrush and onto the trail. They reined in their horses and turned to face the oncoming caravan. Pedro Fernandez rode at its head and, as he approached the brothers, he held up his hand to bring the others to a halt. Then, pulling up his steed, he greeted the Delgados.

'*Buenos días, señores*,' he said.

Luis Delgado smiled.

'*Buenos días*,' he replied, and, pulling one of his two Remingtons out from under his poncho, he promptly shot the trader.

Two slugs ripped into Pedro Fernandez's chest, knocking him out of the saddle. He hit the dusty trail and rolled over, grabbing for his pistol. It was halfway out of his holster when Luis Delgado aimed and fired a third time. The bullet struck Fernandez in the right temple and exploded out of the back of his skull in a shower of blood, brains and splinters of bone. He slumped back and lay still, his sightless eyes staring upwards into the azure-blue sky.

The suddenness of the assault upon their leader took the rest of the caravan completely by surprise. Indeed, they were still in a state of shock when the Delgado brothers began gunning them down.

The brothers went for the six men first, blasting away at them and sending them toppling from their horses. Luis Delgado took two out with single shots to the head. A third he hit in the chest and then the belly. José, meanwhile, emptied one of his two revolvers into the bodies of another pair of Fernandez's followers and shot the sixth man in the back with his other gun as the terrified fellow turned to flee. Not one of the traders had succeeded in drawing his weapon, so swift and unexpected had been the Delgados' attack.

The three women's screams rent the air. Two dropped to their knees beside their fallen husbands and wept unrestrainedly. Maria Fernandez was made of sterner stuff. She crouched down beside her dead spouse and pulled the revolver from his holster. Eyes flashing, she rose and aimed the gun at Luis Delgado, who was checking to see that his fourth victim was indeed dead. She fired. The pistol jolted in her hand, the force of its kick surprising her and almost knocking her off her feet. She had never fired a gun before.

The bullet whistled through the bandit's sombrero, grazing his scalp as it passed. He turned and emptied his second Remington into the woman. The slugs slammed into and through her slender body and, with a cry, she collapsed, to lie spread-eagled across her husband's corpse.

The two brothers grinned wickedly and dismounted. They approached the two wailing women. Suddenly, the women ceased in their lamentations and an eerie silence descended upon the desert.

The next moment, the women were screaming again, as the brothers leapt upon them and ripped the clothes from their bodies.

The sight of his victim's naked white breasts served to increase Luis Delgado's lust. He hastily unbuttoned his trousers and bared himself before her. She gasped and struggled to free herself. But to no avail. A couple of vicious punches to the head dazed her, whereupon Luis brutally forced her legs apart and plunged down on top of her.

The other woman fared no better. José ravished her in similar fashion, cock-a-doodle-do-ing as he reached his climax.

Their animal passions satisfied, the bandits rose and adjusted their clothing. The women, for their part, lay where they had been despoiled, softly moaning. Luis Delgado grinned at his brother and then, pulling the Bowie knife from its sheath, bent down and proceeded to slit the women's throats.

He cleaned the blade on some tumbleweed and slipped it back into the sheath. He fingered the bullet-hole in his sombrero and, tossing it aside, tried on Pedro Fernandez's hat. It did not fit and neither did the next he tried. However, the third man's sombrero fitted him perfectly.

'Now we go to Bonnie Springs, Luis?' said José.

Luis Delgado shook his head.

'No, my brother, we do not go to Bonnie Springs. Not yet,' he replied. 'First we must hide all evidence of this afternoon's work. We do not want it to come to light until we are many miles from here.'

'I suppose not.'

'There is a canyon up yonder in the foothills. We shall hide everyone and everything there. Only then do we go to Bonnie Springs,' said Luis.

And that is what they did. They strapped their victims across the backs of their horses and ponies and led them and the mules up into the foothills. The canyon was small and shallow and situated on the very edge of the desert, but it served to conceal the Delgados and their gruesome caravan from the sight of anyone riding along the Old Spanish Trail.

'Now do we head for Bonnie Springs?' enquired José impatiently.

'We do,' said Luis. 'And we each take with us one mule. No peace officer is likely to suspect a couple of Mexicans trailing mules laden with hand-woven blankets. He will hardly give us a second glance.'

'No, you are right, my brother,' grinned Jose. 'He will simply assume that we are traders taking a much-needed break from our long journey to Los Angeles.'

'And, so, he will be most unlikely to check his Wanted notices.'

'Yes.'

'Let us go, then.'

It took the two bandits a couple of hours to reach the town limits of the small Nevada silver-mining township of Bonnie Springs, nestling beneath the shadow of the nearby mountain. The rendezvous with Sam McCluskey was at the town's one and only saloon, Frenchie's Place. They spotted it halfway down Main Street, on their right-hand side. Before they could reach the saloon, though, they were obliged to pass the law office, on their left-hand side.

Marshal Tim Ryan was sitting in his rocking-chair on the stoop outside, a cheroot clamped between his teeth and the brim of his black, low-crowned Stetson pulled down to shade his eyes. It seemed he was dozing, but appearances can be deceptive. He observed the two Mexicans ride in, just as he or his deputy observed all strangers who rode into Bonnie Springs.

A tall, lean man in his late thirties, with a perpetual sardonic smile and an easy-going manner, Tim Ryan liked to know who was in town. That way, he figured he could avert trouble before it began. He did not expect any from the two Mexicans, however. While most travellers on the Old Spanish Trail tended to break their journey out at Las Vegas, some chose to ride on and stop instead in Bonnie Springs.

Consequently, Ryan assumed that the brothers were merely harmless traders. Luis Delgado's ploy had worked. The marshal didn't even consider checking through his Wanted notices.

The two bandits hitched both their horses and their mules to the rail outside the saloon. Then they climbed the few wooden steps to the stoop and pushed their way in through the batwing doors.

Frenchie's Place was like a hundred or more saloons across the West — but with one exception. It boasted a small stage at its far end, screened by a pair of plush red velvet curtains. Otherwise, it was typical. Brass lamps hung from the rafters, tables and chairs were scattered across the sawdusted floor, there was a pot-bellied stove at either end of the barroom and a spittoon close by the bar-counter with its hammered copper bar-top.

Although there were few customers, there were two bartenders busily polishing glasses behind the bar-counter, three saloon-girls in low-cut dresses displaying their wares and the proprietress leaning nonchalantly against the bar and smoking a cigarette through a long mesquite-wood holder.

Frenchie was a forty-year-old brunette with a still pretty, painted face and a voluptuous figure, her large white breasts almost toppling out of the low-cut bodice of her crimson satin dress. She had been many things in her time. Hailing from the Latin Quarter of New Orleans, she had started out as a waitress in the family restaurant, got bored with that and run off with a gambling man. This liaison had not lasted long and subsequently she had worked as a sporting woman, and then, when her charms faded somewhat, as a madam in a brothel. In this capacity, Frenchie had accumulated sufficient cash to purchase a half-share in Bonnie Springs' sole saloon. The other half-share was held by the town's mayor, but he was quite content to allow Frenchie to run the show.

'*Bonjour, messieurs!*' she cried,

greeting the brothers with her most effusive, professional smile.

This might well have dazzled the Delgados had their gaze not been directed at her ample cleavage.

Luis Delgado eventually succeeded in tearing his eyes away and, returning her smile, replied, '*Buenos días, señora*.'

'You have come far?' she asked.

'Yes, from Santa Fe. We are traders on our way to Los Angeles,' Luis replied.

'You intend to stop over in town this night?'

'Yes, *señora*.'

'Then, you must spend the evening here in my saloon,' Frenchie smiled. 'I can promise you top-class entertainment,' she said.

The brothers glanced across at the three saloon-girls. Frenchie laughed and shook her head.

'No, *messieurs*. That is not what I meant, though, of course, my girls are always at your service. The entertainment I referred to was the show we present every evening at eight o' clock.'

'A show?' said Luis.

'On that stage?' said José, staring towards the plush red velvet curtains.

'Correct. Frenchie's Place proudly presents Bonnie Springs' very own nightingale, the lovely, the melodious Arizona Audrey.'

Frenchie continued to smile widely. Few saloons provided entertainment other than blackjack, or poker, or some other form of gambling. And, certainly, hers was the only one to do so in that particular quarter of Nevada. Consequently, Frenchie's Place attracted not only the citizens of Bonnie Springs, but also those of the various neighbouring townships. Arizona Audrey was an asset Frenchie was most anxious to retain.

'We shall watch your show,' declared Luis Delgado. 'But now it is time to quench our thirsts. It was hot and dusty out on the trail.'

'But, of course, *messieurs*.'

Luis and José Delgado ordered two beers and took them over to a corner table, where it was unlikely their conversation would be overheard. Nevertheless, they conducted it in Spanish and in low tones. José was the first to speak.

'You are sure Señor McCluskey will be here?' he asked.

'Yes, my brother. Sam McCluskey will be here. Sometime today. That is what he said in his wire.'

'And he said it would be worth our while to rendezvous with him, that he had a plan to make us all rich?'

'Yes.'

'But he did not say what that plan was?'

'No.'

'We have ridden a long way, Luis.'

'We have indeed.'

'On the vaguest of promises.'

'That is so. But, José, we have done badly on our own. We have killed many people, yet gained little money. It is my hope that McCluskey's plan will alter that.'

'You really believe he will make us rich?'

‘That is why we are here.’

‘Yes, I suppose it is.’

‘So, drink up, my brother. Tonight we make merry. Tomorrow we make our fortune.’

‘Pray God that we do!’

José crossed himself, then finished his beer in one draught. It had, in truth, been hot and dusty out on the trail.

3

Lanky Oates stared down the barrel of Sheriff Gil Wade's shotgun and blanched. He, Bud Stringer and Jake Berry had ridden into the small desert town of Willow Ford half-an-hour earlier. Now they faced the sheriff across the floor of Danny Parkin's general store.

All three were in their mid-twenties, a bunch of no-account saddle-tramps who rode across the West, preying upon the weak and the vulnerable. They picked their victims with care, tackling only those who they figured were unlikely to put up any kind of resistance. Invariably, their victims were on their own and quite often unarmed. Indeed, during all their nefarious encounters, only once did they shoot anyone. On that occasion, it was Lanky Oates who fired the fatal shot and, even then, there was no face-to-face encounter. He shot his victim in the back.

Tough-looking, unshaven, dusty, thirsty and broke, the three saddle-tramps had ridden into town. They had hitched their broken-down cayuses to the rail outside Danny Parkin's general store and stepped inside. On finding the small, bald-headed, bespectacled storekeeper alone in the store, they had ordered various provisions and, when he had asked them for payment, had laughed in his face.

'Put it on our tab,' Lanky Oates had told him, his hand lingering menacingly above the butt of his Colt Peacemaker.

'But . . . but I don't know you!' Danny Parkin had expostulated.

'You sayin' you don't trust us?'

'No, but . . . '

'No buts, mister. We're takin' these here goods an' there ain't a darned thing you can do about it.'

They had promptly gathered up the provisions and it was as they turned to leave that Oates found himself staring down the barrel of Sheriff Gil Wade's scattergun.

Gil Wade was a slim, dapper thirty-year-old, clad in a grey city-style, three-piece suit and a smart grey Derby hat. His badge of office was clipped to his vest pocket and, like the three saddle-tramps, he carried a Colt Peacemaker in a holster tied down on his right thigh. His grave grey eyes studied Lanky Oates and his companions, while the shotgun remained trained on Oates.

'Figured you boys was up to no good the moment I clapped eyes on you,' remarked the sheriff. 'That's why I moseyed on over here.'

'Praise be to God you did, Gil' exclaimed a relieved Danny Parkin from behind the store counter.

At this point, Lanky Oates decided to try a little bravado, in a desperate attempt to extricate himself and his partners from the awkward situation in which they found themselves.

'Now, look here, Sheriff,' he growled, 'there's three of us an' only one of you.

You cain't hope to out-gun all of us. So, jest step aside or, as sure as eggs is eggs, you're gonna end up dead.'

Sheriff Gil Wade grinned broadly.

'Am I?' he said.

'You surely are.'

'But that won't do you no good.'

'Whaddya mean?'

'You're gonna git both barrels before you or either of your pardners can clear leather.'

Oates carefully considered the sheriff's words. His bravado had failed. The lawman was not about to back down.

'OK,' he said. 'Let's negotiate.'

'What's there to negotiate?' enquired Wade.

'Wa'al, let's say we take only the coffee an' the beef jerky, an' you let us ride outa town? That way, nobody gits hurt.'

'You ain't gonna let the sonofabitch steal my coffee an' . . . ' began Danny Parkin.

'Hell, no!' said Wade.

'So, where does that git us?' demanded Oates.

'It's a goddam stand-off!' exclaimed Bud Stringer.

'That's 'bout it,' agreed Jake Berry.

'I don't think so,' said the sheriff.

'No?' said Oates.

'No. While I hold this gun on you, Danny's at liberty to go fetch my deppities. Then, 'tween us, I reckon we'll easily disarm you an' sling you in the town jail.'

'I . . . I'll go straight away, Gil,' said the storekeeper eagerly.

'Jest a minute!' cried Oates. 'Let's not be too hasty 'bout this. I mean, you an' your deppities try an' arrest us, then someone's certain to git hisself hurt, if not killed.'

'Only if'n you resist arrest.'

'Which we will. Won't we, boys?'

'Er . . . yeah . . . yeah, we sure will,' agreed Bud Stringer and Jake Berry, but without much conviction.

''Course, nobody needs git hurt or killed,' said Oates.

'No?'

'No, Sheriff.' Lanky Oates knew when

he was beaten and he had no intention of risking his life for a few ounces of coffee and a couple of pounds of beef jerky. 'We take nuthin' an' you step aside an' let us go,' he suggested.

Sheriff Gil Wade reflected for some moments. The town jail was already full, for, on the previous evening, there had been a bust-up between some of the townsfolk and the cowboys from a nearby ranch. The protagonists were due to be tried and fined later that afternoon, but, in the meantime . . .

'OK,' he said. 'You boys've got yourselves a deal.'

'Aw, Gil . . . ' began Danny Parkin in protest.

'You want your store shot to pieces?' Wade cut him short.

'Er . . . no. No, guess not.'

'That's settled, then.' Wade again addressed Lanky Oates. 'You an' your pals lam outa town an' don't come back,' he stated firmly.

'OK, if you'd jest lower that there scattergun — '

'Git outa here!' snapped the sheriff
'Jest goin',' said Lanky Oates hastily.
Thereupon, the three saddle-tramps edged away from the store counter and nervously skirted the lawman on their way to the door. Gil Wade, for his part, watched them go, all the while keeping his shotgun aimed at Lanky Oates. He need not have bothered, for, cowards to a man, the trio had no intention of trying anything.

They hurriedly unhitched their cayuses and headed out of town, back onto the trail. They rode southwards.

An hour later, they veered off the trail and made towards the mountains. The trail was surrounded on both sides by desert and they badly needed water. Also, there was a chance they might find game in among the foothills.

They rode steadily onwards, though coming across neither water nor game.

'Hell, Lanky, we ain't gonna make it if'n we don't hit water soon!' gasped Jake Berry.

'Jake's right,' rasped Bud Springer

through parched lips.

'So, whaddya expect me to do 'bout it? I ain't no magician,' retorted Lanky Oates.

'It was your idea for us to ride into that pesky Willow Ford,' said Springer reproachfully.

'It was, too!' added Berry.

'Wa'al, we'd have gotten our provisions if that sheriff hadn't spotted us ridin' into town an' come across to check us out. Most peace officers wouldn't have bothered. We was plain unlucky,' said Oates. ''Sides, Willow Ford was the only town within a twenty-mile radius. So, where in blue blazes did you fellers expect me to take you?'

'Hmm. S'pose you've got a point there,' muttered Springer.

'Darned right I have!' declared Oates.

The other two made no further comments and the trio rode on in a surly silence.

It was a good hour later when, as they made their way round the rock-strewn base of a large mesa, Bud Springer suddenly cried out.

'Holy cow!' he yelled. 'I do declare I smell coffee!'

Both Lanky Oates and Jake Berry sniffed the air.

'Goddammit, you're right!' exclaimed Lanky Oates.

They spurred on their horses and, skirting a tumble of boulders, came upon the source of the coffee-smell.

A man had built and lit a small campfire in the shade of the mesa. And there, out of the heat of the blazing afternoon sun, he was quietly enjoying some beef jerky and a mug of steaming hot coffee. The coffee-pot continued to bubble away on the campfire. To the three saddle-tramps it smelled delicious. They immediately reined in their horses.

The man looked up and smiled.

'Howdy, fellers!' he said, adding, 'it's sure mighty hot out there.' He indicated the desert with a sweep of his arm.

'It darned well is!' agreed Lanky

Oates, and he studied the stranger thoughtfully. The man was no spring chicken, probably in his late fifties or early sixties. He was small, bespectacled and scrawny-looking, with a thin, foxy face. Straggly white hair escaped from beneath the brim of his tall black stovepipe hat and he sprouted white whiskers beneath his narrow, pointed nose. His jaw, however, was clean-shaven. A white cambric shirt, black bootlace tie and light grey vest could be seen beneath his black Prince Albert coat. Light grey trousers and black leather boots completed his apparel.

Oates noted that the man carried a British Tranter, its pearl handle protruding from the holster tied down on his right thigh. He also noted the neat gold chain leading into one of the man's vest pockets. He concluded that it was likely attached to a gold hunter.

'You fellers are welcome to help yourselves to some coffee,' said the old man. ''Fraid I'm outa vittels, though,' he added, chewing the last lump of the beef jerky.

'Coffee'd be fine,' said Lanky Oates. 'We're obliged to you.'

He and his two companions dismounted, produced tin mugs from their saddle-bags and helped themselves from the coffee-pot. The coffee was good and strong, and very welcome after their dusty ride in the heat of the afternoon sun.

'You boys travellin' far?' enquired the stranger.

'Jest bummin' around. Ain't headin' nowhere in partickler, are we, fellers?' said Oates, glancing at the other two.

'Nope. Jest wanderin',' agreed Bud Stringer.

' 'S right,' said Jake Berry.

'What about you, mister?' said Oates, and he fixed the small, thin figure huddled over the campfire with a speculative eye.

'Me? Aw, I gotta rendezvous to keep!' replied the man.

'Yeah?'

'Yup. First light tomorrow.'

'A business meetin'?'

'I guess you could call it that.'

Oates grinned. He had guessed as much. The city-style clothes indicated that the man was some kind of businessman, probably from one of the East Coast cities, extending his interests into the West.

'I thought so,' said Oates.

'What sort of business you in, mister?' asked Stringer curiously.

'Private business.'

Stringer scowled.

'You ain't gonna tell us?' he said.

'That's right; I ain't,' retorted the little man.

'That ain't very friendly.'

'It's as friendly as I git. I offered y'all some coffee, but I sure as hell ain't gonna tell you my business.'

Oates noted the hard edge that had crept into the stranger's tone. He smiled a conciliatory smile.

'Reckon that's your right,' he said smoothly.

'Yup,' said the old man.

Stringer continued to scowl, while Jake Berry shot an enquiring glance at the smiling Lanky Oates. Oates was not usually quite so reasonable.

'Whatever your business is, I'd say it was pretty darned profitable,' Oates remarked.

'An' jest why would you suppose that?' asked the stranger.

''Cause you're pretty neatly attired an', if that chain's anythin' to go by, you're carryin' a gold hunter in your vest pocket.'

'Correct.'

'Wa'al, gold hunters don't come cheap.'

'This one did.'

'Huh?'

'It was handed down to me by my pappy.'

'Oh!'

'Yeah. An' he got it from his pappy who, in turn . . . wa'al, you git the picture.'

'You're sayin' it's a family heirloom?'

'Exactly.'

The old man pulled forth the watch and showed it to the three young saddle-tramps. Then he returned it to the vest pocket.

'That'd fetch quite a few bucks,' said Oates. 'If 'n you was to sell it.'

'But I ain't got no intention of sellin' it,' said the old man.

'No, but I have.'

'I beg your pardon?'

'I intend to sell it.'

''T'ain't yours to sell.'

'It will be when you hand it over.'

'An' jest why would I do that?'

''Cause, if you don't, me an' my pardners'll kill you. Won't we, boys?'

Bud Stringer's scowl promptly changed into an evil leer and Jake Berry laughed harshly.

'We sure will, Lanky,' said Stringer.

'Yeah. Why not?' said Berry.

'You fellers must be mighty hard up,' commented the stranger.

'We are,' said Oates.

'Even so. Surely you wouldn't rob an

old man of his one an' only heirloom?'

'We don't know that's your one an' only heirloom.'

'I'm tellin' you.'

'Too bad! We want it, old man.'

'Yeah. An', if you know what's good for you, you'll jest hand it over nice 'n' easy,' said Stringer.

'We don't wanta have to shoot you,' added Oates,

'That's good,' said the little old man, ''cause you ain't gonna.'

'Ain't gonna have to, y'mean?' said Oates.

'No,' the stranger corrected him. 'Ain't gonna.'

The pearl-handled British Tranter cleared leather in the twinkling of an eye, before any of the three saddle-tramps could make a move.

The first shot hit Lanky Oates in the chest and sent him crashing backwards, to land flat on his back among the hoofs of his and his partners' horses. The horses whinnied and backed away.

The second and third shots followed

in quick succession. Bud Stringer was struck plumb in the centre of his forehead before he could even reach the butt of his Colt Peacemaker. Jake Berry had drawn his revolver halfway out of its holster when he was hit by the stranger's third shot. It took out his left eye and ricocheted up into his brain.

Both Bud Stringer and Jake Berry died instantly. Lanky Oates, on the other hand, was seriously, but not mortally, wounded. He lay in the dust, his left hand clasped to the wound in his chest, while his right hand closed round his gun-butt.

'I wouldn't bother,' said the stranger.

He pushed the wire-framed spectacles back onto the bridge of his nose and peered down at the wounded saddle-tramp. Lanky Oates released his grip on the gun. The colour had faded from his cheeks and the blood from the chest wound was beginning to ooze out from between his fingers. He glared up at the little old man whom he had so badly underestimated.

‘Who . . . who in tarnation are you?’ he gasped.

‘The name’s J. C. Sharkey,’ replied the other.

‘Jeeze!’

J. C. Sharkey permitted himself a wintry smile.

‘You’ve heard of me?’ he asked.

‘You’re a goddam legend,’ replied Oates.

‘Yes.’

‘That . . . that gold hunter. Is it really a family heirloom?’

Sharkey laughed.

‘Hell, no!’ he said. ‘I took it off a feller I shot in Wichita. ’Bout five, six years back.’

‘Goddammit!’

‘Yeah. Wa’al, that’s the way it goes,’ said J. C. Sharkey, and he pointed his revolver at the supine Lanky Oates and shot him between the eyes.

4

Phineas Yeats' room in the Bonnie Springs Hotel overlooked Main Street. Jack Stone stood at the window, looking out across the street at the saloon opposite. It was early evening, lamps had been lit and oblongs of yellow light spilled out from the front door and windows of Frenchie's Place. As Stone watched, two riders reined in before the saloon, dismounted and hitched their horses to the rail outside. The two men, one tall and broad-shouldered, the other slim and of medium height, hurried up the steps onto the stoop and vanished through the batwing doors. Neither man realized he was being watched by the big Kentuckian. Stone, for his part, viewed the pair idly and without any real interest. He did not recognize either of them. He turned to face the Pinkerton man.

Phineas Yeats lay upon the hotel bed, fully dressed apart from his grey Derby hat. He had been seen by the doctor and his wound had been cleaned, dressed and bandaged. The bandage was wrapped tight round his upper torso and, consequently, he felt much as he expected a woman did in her corset. He was wearing a fresh white shirt to replace the one Stone had earlier torn up to plug and bind the wound.

'How are you feelin'?' enquired Stone.

'I've felt better,' grunted the Pinkerton man.

'Wa'al, you've only got yourself to blame.'

'You fired the shot that — '

'We've already discussed that. You got what you deserved. 'Deed, you're lucky I didn't shoot to kill.'

'Hmm. Wa'al . . . yeah . . . guess so,' agreed Yeats reluctantly.

'So, what are your plans for tomorrow? You can scarcely pursue Sam

McCluskey the way you are.'

'Nope.'

'So?'

'I've been thinkin' 'bout that. I could telegraph Chicago an' git them to send another agent to meet me here in Bonnie Springs.' Yeats frowned and then continued, 'But there don't seem much point, seein' as how I've lost track of the sonofabitch. Therefore, I guess I'll head back to Chicago.'

'Your boss won't be pleased.'

'I ain't none too pleased myself. But, hell, McCluskey could be anywhere by now! All I know for sure is that he rode south from Cherry Creek a few days back.'

'Wa'al, if I was you, I'd wire Chicago an' explain matters, an' ask them for instructions. Then it'll be their decision whether or not to send another agent.'

'You're right, Jack. I'll git a wire off straight away.'

'An' after you've done that?'

'What d'you suggest?'

'I could eat a hoss.'

'So, we find some place to eat?'

'Yup. Then, if'n you're up to it, I reckon we might mosey along to Frenchie's Place.'

'Frenchie's Place?'

'The town's only saloon. I strolled in there while you was bein' tended to by the doc.'

'Oh, yeah?'

'Yeah. An' it seems they have some kinda show each night. Draws folks in from all the neighbourin' townships.'

'OK, Jack. When we've eaten, we'll give Frenchie's Place the benefit of our custom,' declared the Pinkerton man.

The show was almost certainly sure to feature several scantily-clad young women and, while his wound precluded him from doing anything other than look at them, nevertheless Phineas Yeats felt the sight of the girls singing and dancing on stage would unquestionably cheer him up.

It was only with Stone's help, however, that he managed to rise from the bed. Thereupon, donning his hat, he followed the Kentuckian out of the room, downstairs and out into Main Street.

Meanwhile, the two men Stone had observed entering the saloon were at the bar-counter, thirstily gulping back great draughts of beer. It had been a long, dusty ride to Bonnie Springs.

The bigger of the two was attired in a brown Stetson, check shirt, brown leather vest, denim pants and well-worn, un-spurred boots. He carried a Remington in his holster. Ice-cold, pitiless black eyes stared out of an ugly, weather-beaten and pock-marked visage. Sam McCluskey was no oil painting.

The other man, slim and elegant in his black three-piece, city-style suit and Derby hat, also carried a gun, but not in a holster on his thigh. A long-barrelled .30 calibre Colt nestled in a shoulder rig concealed beneath his jacket. It was there for reasons of self-defence and had not, so far, been used. He was a gambling man, rather than a gunman. Twinkling blue eyes and a ready smile signalled that Slim Jim Linn was a man with both a zest for life and a sense of humour.

'So, where in tarnation are the others?' he enquired.

'They'll be here.'

'I sure hope so.'

'Them two brothers ain't gonna miss out on this.'

'Whatever it is.'

'Whaddya mean?'

'Wa'al,' said Slim Jim Linn, 'we don't none of us know *what* the set-up is.'

Sam McCluskey lowered his voice to a whisper.

'J. C. Sharkey don't plan no small-scale job. This is gonna be a real big 'un, I can tell you.'

'Yeah, wa'al . . . '

'Here they are now, Slim Jim.'

The gambler turned to see the Delgado brothers push their way into the saloon through the batwing doors. Having quenched their thirst earlier, the two Mexicans had gone off in search of something to eat. They had subsequently eaten in a cantina on the opposite side of the street and now were returning to the appointed rendezvous, Frenchie's Place.

'Luis? José?' said McCluskey.

'Sam Mc . . . ?' began Luis Delgado.

'Jest plain Sam,' McCluskey snarled, cutting him short.

'Ah, yes, *señor*!'

'An' this here's Slim Jim.'

'Nice to meet you, Señor Slim Jim.'

'An' you,' replied the gambler courteously, although this was not strictly true. He was beginning to have doubts about the entire enterprise.

McCluskey ordered four beers and they retired to a corner table. The show was due to commence in just under the hour, and he wanted to get their business discussion concluded before there was any chance of it being overheard. This meant they had to be both quick and brief, since the saloon was rapidly filling. Arizona Audrey and her girls were evidently a popular attraction.

'OK, fellers,' said McCluskey, 'I'll tell you how come I asked y'all to meet here in Bonnie Springs.'

'Yes?' said Luis Delgado.

'You have heard of J. C. Sharkey, I s'pose?' he asked of the brothers.

They both nodded and José said, 'The bank robber. He is, how you say . . . very famous.'

'Notorious,' Slim Jim corrected him.

'Anyways, him an' me met up in Jackson County Jail,' said McCluskey. 'We was talkin' one day 'bout this an' that, an' J.C. said — '

'J.C?' enquired José, puzzled.

'Everyone refers to J. C. Sharkey as jest J.C. Dunno what those initials stand for. Don't much matter really.'

'No.'

'So, as I was sayin', J.C. an' me was talkin' an' he said that his last bank raid, the one he was doin' time for, only went wrong 'cause his gang wasn't up to it. He'd recruited 'em in a hurry an' none of 'em was worth a red cent.'

McCluskey paused and eyed each of his companions in turn before continuing, 'J.C. declared that next time he'd make no such mistake. He'd be darned sure to pick the best bunch he could find. So, I asked him who he had in mind. An' guess what he said?'

'You tell us, *señor*,' replied Luis Delgado.

'Wa'al, he said he had a bank job in view, which'd make him, an' whoever rode with him, rich for life. He reckoned he'd need four men, three who were good with a gun an' one who could blow open a safe.'

'He . . . he was expectin' there to be some shootin', then?' interjected Slim Jim Linn nervously.

'Nope. Like I already told you, Slim Jim, J.C. plans this job to be nice 'n' easy. But, jest in case things go wrong, he wants fellers along who can shoot their way outa trouble.'

'Which is why he chose you, Señor McCluskey?' said Luis Delgado.

'Yup. An' that's also why he chose

you an' your brother. You boys have one helluva reputation.'

'And the other gringo?' said José Delgado, glancing across at the gambler.

'Aw, Slim Jim's 'bout the best doggone safe-blower in the entire West!' stated McCluskey.

'Indeed?'

José eyed the gambler speculatively, as did his elder brother.

'I'm flattered J.C. should think so highly of me,' said Slim Jim modestly.

In fact, he had every reason to be modest. His reputation was based on the one and only bank raid he had ever been involved in, a bank raid that had gone seriously wrong. He had been broke at the time and had allowed himself to be persuaded by a lunkhead by the name of Fats Bentley to participate in the raid. In the absence of anyone in the gang who knew how to blow open a safe, Bentley had delegated this task to Slim Jim. By pure luck, he had used exactly the right quantity of dynamite and had succeeded in making a perfect job of it. Unfortunately, thereafter matters had gone badly wrong. An horrendous shoot-out had followed and the rest of Fats Bentley's gang had been shot dead, only Bentley and Slim Jim surviving. They had escaped together, but shortly afterwards parted. Slim Jim Linn's reputation as a safe-blower, however, was established. Fats Bentley, anxious to promote his own reputation as a daring desperado, had given every outlaw he had met a glamorized and wholly fictitious version of the failed bank raid and, in so doing, had naturally boasted of his astuteness in recruiting a safe-blower of Slim Jim's calibre.

'J.C. got it wrong last time,' said Luis Delgado, as he continued to eye the gambler.

'Are . . . are you implyin' that I . . . ?' began Slim Jim.

'Luis is implyin' nuthin',' rasped McCluskey. 'Are you?' he asked the Mexican pointedly.

'Well, *señor* . . .'

'J.C. had all the time in the world to pick his gang. I figure he's picked the best,' said McCluskey. No false modesty there.

The two brothers shrugged their shoulders.

'OK,' said Luis.

'We, J.C. an' me, fixed things jest 'fore I was released. He had another three months to do. In that time I was to find an' recruit you three,' explained McCluskey.

'It was easy to find us?' enquired José.

'Pretty darned easy. You two leave everywhere you go littered with a heap of corpses. Guess you're wanted in almost every goddam state in the Union. It took several enquiries, but I eventually tracked you down to that well-known refuge for outlaws, Providence Flats.'

'Yes. And you wired us to meet you here today at Bonnie Springs, in Frenchie's Place. Why here?'

‘’Cause those were J.C.’s orders. Slim Jim I found in Reno an’ we rode here together.’

‘That’s right,’ concurred the gambler.

‘So, this J. C. Sharkey, he will arrive tonight?’ said Luis.

‘No. We book into the Bonnie Springs Hotel. He will rendezvous with us there at first light tomorrow. We gotta be up an’ ready to ride out straight away,’ said McCluskey.

‘Then, it is not the bank in Bonnie Springs that we plan to raid?’

‘Guess not.’

‘So, where is this bank that holds sufficient funds to make all five of us rich for life?’

‘I dunno.’

‘You do not know!’ Luis Delgado sounded astonished.

‘You heard me.’

‘But . . . ’

‘J.C.’s playin’ this one close to his chest.’

‘Mebbe he’s scared if ’n he tells us what he has in mind, we’ll jest go ahead an' pull off the job without him,' suggested Slim Jim.

'Could be,' acknowledged McCluskey.

'Well, it has been a long, hard ride from Providence Flats. I hope José and I have not wasted our time,' said Luis.

'You can trust J.C. Your ride will surely prove to have been worthwhile,' declared McCluskey confidently.

By this time, they had finished their beers and the big outlaw rose and went to fetch four more, while Slim Jim handed round cigars.

They were onto their third round of beers and the bar-room was packed to capacity when eight o'clock struck and the plush red velvet curtains parted to reveal the voluptuous, satin-clad figure of the saloon keeper, Frenchie.

'*Mesdames, messieurs*,' she cried, 'Frenchie's Place proudly presents the finest all-singing, all-dancing show in the state of Nevada, featuring Bonnie Springs' very own nightingale, the beautiful, the melodious Arizona Audrey and *Les Girls*.'

At this, she stepped aside, a honky-tonk piano and two fiddles struck up and Arizona Audrey and four scantily-clad young brunettes bounced onto the small stage. Audrey belted out, 'See What the Boys in the Back Room Will Have', in a slightly off-key warble while, behind her, the girls executed a non-too-expert dance routine involving a series of high kicks. The audience applauded wildly and roared their delight at the sight of the dancers' long, slender legs, their frilly knickers and their firm white breasts almost popping out of the low-cut bodices of their colourful costumes. Visions in blue, green, mauve and yellow danced back and forth across the boards, while Arizona Audrey held centre stage in a gown of bright scarlet.

Audrey was a petite bottle-blonde in her mid-thirties, pretty rather than beautiful, with mischievous brown eyes, an upturned nose and a perpetually cheeky grin. And, although her gown was full-length, it had a split up to her thigh and was so décolleté that her cleavage left very little to the imagination. Her breasts were small and firm like those of the four dancers and, when she bowed at the end of each song, the applause was truly deafening.

From off-stage Frenchie smiled happily.

Indeed, everyone in the saloon seemed to be having a good time, with the single exception of Sam McCluskey. He had tugged forward his Stetson to shade the upper half of his face, and his mouth was fixed in a ferocious scowl. Slim Jim stared at him curiously.

'What the hell's the matter, Sam?' he enquired.

'Arizona Audrey's the matter,' he replied in a low growl.

'Arizona Audrey! Why she's a darned good — '

'She knows me.'

'What?'

'From a few years back. In Abilene. She was jest plain Audrey then an' was a saloon-girl at Ferdie Baines' Hot

Dollar Saloon. Ferdie employed me to protect his premises. It was my job to deal with any troublemakers. Me an' Audrey, we worked there day in, day out, for 'bout a year. Then I had to lam it outa town in a hurry on account of I shot a feller. Unfortunately, he happened to be the deppity sheriff.'

'Jeeze!'

'But so what, Señor Sam? You are not now a wanted man,' said Luis Delgado.

'That's right,' said Slim Jim. 'You served your time. Why, it's a mere three months since you was released from jail.'

'I was never jailed for that killin', though. 'Sides, some weeks ago I shot another feller. This time durin' a hold-up.'

'You did what?' Slim Jim looked aghast.

'I needed the money. Was I s'posed to exist on thin air till J.C. finally got his release?' McCluskey glanced at the Delgado brothers. 'I ain't the only one on the run. You boys are, too. Right?'

'That is true,' admitted Luis.

'But the marshal here in Bonnie Springs, he suspected nothing when we rode in,' said José.

'No?'

'No. We brought with us mules laden with hand-woven blankets. Naturally, he took us for honest traders heading north.'

'How . . . how did you come by the blankets an' the mules?' enquired Slim Jim uneasily.

'We borrowed them,' said Luis, and he favoured the gambler with a wicked leer.

Slim Jim groaned. Once again he was broke. Which was why he had let Sam McCluskey persuade him to join Sharkey's gang. Now, he was beginning to wish he hadn't. The Delgado brothers scared him. They were truly evil.

At this point, Arizona Audrey burst forth into another song, effectively silencing them. They waited until the song was concluded before resuming their conversation. With the audience again stomping, clapping and hollering wildly, nobody was likely to pick up a word they said. In fact, although they stuck their heads close together, the four had trouble hearing themselves speak.

'If Arizona Audrey spots me an' informs the marshal, we're done for,' remarked McCluskey gloomily.

'So, we must make sure she don't,' said Slim Jim.

'But how?'

Luis Delgado grinned and drew a finger across his throat. The gambler shuddered and shook his head.

'Too risky,' he said.

'I agree,' said McCluskey.

'You could simply lie low until first light tomorrow,' suggested Slim Jim.

'An' if she should see me as we ride forth with J.C?' McCluskey frowned and said, 'No — we need to git her outa town.'

'We kidnap her, then?' said Luis Delgado.

'Again too risky.'

'But, Señor Sam . . . '

'It's gotta be done quietly. She must be persuaded to . . . ' McCluskey paused, thought hard for some moments, then suddenly said, 'Say some theatre impressario from 'Frisco . . . or mebbe Noo York even, was to turn up here an' offer her a contract? You could pose as one of them fellers, Slim Jim. 'Deed, you look the part.'

'Oh, no!' said Slim Jim.

'Oh, yeah!' said McCluskey. 'Go hire a hoss an' gig an' git yourself out the back of the saloon. Then, when the show's over, step inside an' persuade Arizona Audrey to take a ride with you.'

'Where to, for Pete's sake?'

'I'll leave that up to you. Use your imagination. Jest make sure it sounds convincin'.'

'Then . . . then what?'

'Take her out into the mountains an' shoot her.'

'Sh . . . shoot her?'

''Course. We need to git rid of her

permanently. Only make certain you hide her body real good. We don't want it found till we're well away from here. OK?'

It was certainly *not* OK, but Slim Jim realized he had no choice in the matter.

'Hirin' a hoss an' gig costs money,' he said.

Sam McCluskey slapped a wad of dollar bills into the gambler's hand.

'Slip out at the end of her next number,' he whispered as the applause died down and Arizona Audrey and *Les Girls* embarked upon their next routine.

Slim Jim did as Sam McCluskey bade him. Hiring the horse and gig proved easy enough. Slim Jim presented a respectable figure, and the ostler at the livery stables happily swallowed his tale that he needed to ride over to nearby Overton to pick up his ailing mother.

The next part was likely to prove rather trickier. Slim Jim waited at the back of the saloon for the show to end and, while he did so, rehearsed what he was going to say to Arizona Audrey. Eventually, when he stepped in through the rear door, he was pretty well word-perfect. He prayed that the saloon-singer would be convinced by his performance.

Fortune favoured the gambler. When Slim Jim stepped inside, he found Arizona Audrey backstage and alone. Frenchie was out front chatting to her customers and *Les Girls*, having entertained the men with their high kicking dance routines, were now offering to entertain them rather more intimately in the saloon's upstairs bedrooms. The showgirls had reverted to being sporting women.

Audrey sat on a high-backed wooden chair, her head in her hands. It was always the same. At the end of every performance, she felt emotionally and physically drained. She needed some little time on her own, and in peace and quiet, to recover. Frenchie understood this and invariably left her undisturbed. She would join the others in the bar-room later, when she felt able.

'I enjoyed your performance,' said Slim Jim Linn amiably.

The blonde looked up.

'Do . . . do I know you, sir?' she enquired.

'Nope. I'm a stranger in these parts.'

'Thought I hadn't seen you around.'

'Jerome Muggeridge at your service.'

'You lookin' for Frenchie?'

'No. I was lookin' for you.'

'Me?'

'Yeah. I represent Mr Rupert G. Barnaby. You'll have heard of him, of course?'

'Er . . . no, Mr Muggeridge, can't say I have.'

'But you're in the business!' Slim Jim pretended to be surprised.

'What business?' asked Audrey, mystified.

'Show business.'

'Ah!'

'Mr Barnaby owns no fewer than three theatres.'

'He does?'

'Yes. In Noo York.'

The blonde's eyes lit up.

'In Noo York, you say?'

'That's right, Miss Audrey.'

'An' you're his representative?'

'Exactly. Y'see, Mr Barnaby is forever lookin' for noo talent. Indeed, he is currently travellin' across America, from sea to shinin' sea, in search of it.'

'He is?'

'Certainly. Every so often he picks some place to stop. Then I go out an' canvas the area round about for any homespun talent. When I find someone who I think might fit the bill, a singer, or a dancer, or a comedian, say, I bring him or her along to where Mr Barnaby's stayin' for an audition. So far, Mr Barnaby has picked out a dozen or so entertainers who he's despatched to Noo York with instructions that they be employed in one or other of his theatres.'

'Wow!' Audrey was by now quite excited. She gazed eagerly at the gambler and said, 'An' you came to

Bonnie Springs lookin' for me?'

'I did. Heard 'bout the show here at Frenchie's Place an' figured it might be worth watchin'.'

'An' what's your verdict?'

'I think you've got what it takes, Miss Audrey.'

'Really!' Audrey looked positively radiant. All sign of weariness had gone.

'Really. So, I've taken the liberty of bringin' my gig round to the rear door, hopin' you'll agree to come with me an' be auditioned by Mr Barnaby.'

'I . . . I don't know, Mr Muggeridge.'

'You don't know? But this is your big chance!'

'Look, Frenchie is a good friend of mine. I cain't jest run off without a word. Let me go tell her what you — '

'No, there ain't no need.'

'No need?'

'Not yet. I mean, we don't know for sure that Mr Barnaby will wanta take you on.'

'True.'

'So, why not come an' do your

audition, an' then, if Mr Barnaby wants you, return an' tell Miss Frenchie? If 'n he don't, I'll bring you back an' you say nuthin'. She need never know that you was thinkin' of leavin'.'

'That seems a li'l sneaky.'

'Not at all. Jest plain common sense.'

'Hmm. Wa'al, where is your Mr Barnaby stayin', anyway?'

'At the Paradise Hotel, Boulder City.'

'I see.'

Arizona Audrey gave the matter some thought. Boulder City was only a few miles away. She could be there and back by breakfast-time the next morning. And Mr Muggeridge was right. This was her big chance. She felt guilty about deceiving Frenchie, yet she knew she would regret it for the rest of her life if she didn't at least try. Should she fail, she could always tell Frenchie the next day that she had had a raging headache and, consequently, had slipped home to bed.

'Wa'al?' said Slim Jim.

'OK. Let's go,' replied Audrey.

Slim Jim smiled. But it was an artificial smile. He was far from happy with his lot. For two pins, he would have high-tailed it out of Bonnie Springs, never to return. But, if he did so, he feared Sam McCluskey and the Delgado brothers would come looking for him. And, when they found him . . . he shuddered.

'Are you cold, Mr Muggeridge?' asked Arizona Audrey.

'Er . . . no, no.'

'But you shivered.'

'A touch of my old ague,' he lied.

The gambler had, some years earlier, stayed at the Paradise Hotel in Boulder City. He knew the town was in the vicinity, but had no clear recollection as to whether it lay north, south, east or west of Bonnie Springs. He headed north.

The night was dark and, anyway, Audrey was preoccupied with the thought that she might one day star on the New York stage. She besieged Slim Jim with questions about the city and its theatres. Fortunately, he had for a spell lived in the city and, so, was able to answer all her questions truthfully and without any hesitation.

In this manner, they journeyed northwards along the Old Spanish Trail for several miles, before veering off towards the mountains. They were travelling through the foothills when, all at once, Audrey exclaimed, 'Surely we should've reached Boulder City by now?'

Slim Jim Linn reined in the horse and brought the gig to a halt.

'Why . . . why have we stopped?' she asked, suddenly anxious.

''Cause this is as far as we're goin',' replied the gambler.

'But this ain't Boulder City. Hell, it's in the middle of nowhere!'

'That's right. We're in the mountains 'bout twenty-five miles north of Bonnie Springs.' Slim Jim pulled out the .30 calibre Colt from inside his jacket and brandished it beneath the singer's pretty, upturned nose. 'Git down outa this gig, please.'

A pale-faced Arizona Audrey stepped out of the gig, followed quickly by her abductor. She turned to face him.

'You ain't no theatrical representative,' she said.

'No.'

'An' your name ain't Jerome Muggeridge.'

'No.'

'So, why'd you lie to me?'

'I needed to git you outa Bonnie Springs.'

'But why?'

Slim Jim debated with himself for a moment or two, then decided to tell her the truth, or as much of it as he felt was necessary.

'An ol' pal of yourn is in town.'

'So?'

'He's wanted by the law. He was afraid you'd recognize him an' mebbe alert the marshal.'

'Who . . . who is this ol' pal?'

'Sam McCluskey.'

'That murderin' sonofabitch! Six years ago in Abilene he went an' shot the deppity sheriff.'

'I know.'

'In the back.'

'I didn't know that.'

'So, what're you gonna do? Shoot me?'

'Those were Sam's instructions. But I ain't never shot nobody in my life an' I ain't plannin' to start now.'

'Oh, thank God!' Audrey's relief was palpable. 'What *are* you gonna do, then?' she asked nervously.

'I'm gonna leave you here,' said Slim Jim. 'Sam an' me, we're quittin' town at first light, an' I don't reckon you'll make it back before mid-mornin' at the earliest.'

He crossed his fingers as he said this. J. C. Sharkey had decreed that they would meet at first light and ride out straight away. He was relying upon the bank robber to be punctual.

'You sayin' I've gotta walk all the way back to Bonnie Springs?' exclaimed Audrey.

'That's about it,' he said, adding with

a grin, 'Unless you're gonna sprout wings an' fly.'

He climbed back into the gig, shoved the long-barrelled revolver back into the shoulder rig and, with a flick of the reins, urged the horse into a trot. Moments later, the gig had circled round and was heading back the way it had come.

Arizona Audrey stared disconsolately after the carriage until, eventually, it disappeared into the night. Then she squared her shoulders and told herself to brighten up, that she was lucky to be alive. If Sam McCluskey had driven her out into the desert, he would have shot her for sure. She was heartily thankful, therefore, that he had delegated that task to the man calling himself Jerome Muggeridge.

She set off in relatively good heart, singing as she strode along, in a valiant attempt to keep up her spirits. A couple of miles down the trail, she removed her bright scarlet dancing shoes and continued barefoot. By this time, she was no longer singing.

It was a long, hard slog. She stumbled on through the foothills, hoping to regain the Old Spanish Trail, but unable to find it in the darkness. The stillness of the night was pierced from time to time by the eerie howls of coyotes. These caused the hairs on the back of Audrey's neck to rise and her pace to quicken. But not for long, for her feet were by now both badly bruised and bloodied. The march slackened to a walk and the walk to a shuffle.

At first light Audrey spotted the Old Spanish Trail approximately one mile away to her left across the desert. Fifty yards ahead stood the mouth of a small canyon and, above it, Audrey observed several buzzards circling. Despite her sore feet, the blonde's curiosity got the better of her and she decided to investigate. She staggered into the mouth of the canyon, where, to her horror, she came upon the half-eaten corpses of Pedro Fernandez and his band of Mexican traders.

5

Dawn was breaking as J. C. Sharkey rode his sorrel mare across the town limits and down Main Street towards the Bonnie Springs Hotel.

From inside the law office, Marshal Tim Ryan watched him trot slowly past. The lawman was enjoying his first mug of coffee of the day. He smiled benignly at the sight of the small, blackclad figure with his tall stovepipe hat, and lit a cheroot. Then he returned to his chair behind the desk and dismissed the little man from his mind. There was little likelihood, Ryan reckoned, that the stranger would cause any trouble. In this he was right, but only because Sharkey had planned his raid elsewhere.

There were four horses hitched to the rail outside the hotel. Of the Delgado brothers' mules there was no sign. Both the beasts and their burdens of hand-woven blankets were in the town's livery stables, where the Mexicans intended to leave them. They had served their purpose and now could be safely abandoned.

As Sharkey rode up to the hotel, the front door opened and the huge figure of Sam McCluskey stepped across the threshold into the early-morning sunlight. He was closely followed by Slim Jim Linn and the Delgado brothers.

Sharkey did not bother to dismount. He greeted them from the saddle.

'Mornin', gents.'

'Mornin', J.C.,' replied McCluskey.

The others stared at him open-mouthed. They had all heard of J. C. Sharkey. The man was indeed a legend. But none of them had ever seen him, and he was not how any of them had imagined him. With his stovepipe hat, straggly white hair and moustache, wire-framed spectacles and black Prince Albert coat, he looked more like an elderly mortician than a desperado.

'You fellers lost your tongues?' he enquired tartly.

'S . . . sorry! Mornin', Mr Sharkey,' said Slim Jim.

'Yes. *Buenos días*, Señor Sharkey,' chorused the brothers.

'Jest call me J.C.,' said Sharkey. 'So long as you remember I'm boss, you can cut out the 'mister'.'

'OK . . . J.C.,' said Luis Delgado, grinning broadly.

'An' you are?' asked Sharkey.

'Luis.'

'Good to meet you, Luis. An' you, too, José.' He turned to face the gambler. 'An' you must be Slim Jim Linn. Fats Bentley sure spoke well of you. Reckoned you're the tops with dynamite, that you can crack a safe as sweet as a nut.'

'Yeah, I guess I got the knack,' lied Slim Jim.

'Wa'al, I got the dynamite, some fulminate caps, a roll of sticky tape an' a length of fuse stashed away neat an' tidy in one of my saddle-bags,' said

Sharkey, adding, 'I wasn't sure how many sticks you'd need, so I played it safe an' brought half-a-dozen.'

'Perfect,' said Slim Jim, feverishly racking his brain to remember how many sticks he had used in his one and only attempt at safe blowing.

'Slim Jim has other uses,' interjected McCluskey, and he went on to relate how the gambler had lured Arizona Audrey away from Bonnie Springs, to prevent her spotting him and informing the law. 'Took her out into the desert an' shot her dead, didn't you?' he added.

'Yup. Jest like you told me to,' averred Slim Jim.

'So, the law around here didn't recognize you, Sam?' said Sharkey.

'Nope,' replied McCluskey.

'Or you two?'

The Delgado brothers shook their heads.

'We all slipped into town nice 'n' easy, an', since we've been here, we ain't done nuthin' to rouse anyone's suspicions,' said McCluskey.

'Good!'

'You plannin' on raidin' the bank here in Bonnie Springs?'

'Nope.'

'Then, where you got in mind, J.C.?'

'Flagstaff, Arizona.'

'But, hell, that's 'bout two hundred miles south of here!'

'That's right, Sam. If'n we set out straight away, I figure we'll git there sometime Friday mornin'.'

'But why Flagstaff?'

''Cause on this comin' Saturday the town holds its annual hoss fair, the biggest goddam hoss fair in the whole of the state of Arizona. There'll be real big money there an' I reckon a fair amount of it'll be deposited in the bank for safe keepin'.'

'So, *that's* the bank you're plannin' to raid?'

'Correct, Sam. I ain't quite finalized my plans yet. I'll do that when I've given the town the once-over. That's why I aim to arrive there on Friday.'

‘Good thinkin’, J.C.’

‘So, if you fellers’d care to mount up. We’ll be on our way.’

‘OK.’

The four stepped down off the stoop and quickly unhitched and mounted their horses. A couple of minutes later, all five were cantering down Main Street. They left Bonnie Springs from the end opposite to that by which J. C. Sharkey had entered the town. Consequently, they did not have to pass the law office and, therefore, were not observed by Marshal Tim Ryan as he stood peering out of the window while sipping his second mug of coffee.

Slim Jim Linn had been right. It was mid-morning, almost four hours after the outlaws’ departure, when Arizona Audrey finally staggered, footsore and weary, into Bonnie Springs. Her scarlet dress was soaked with sweat and covered in red dust, her blonde hair was uncharacteristically bedraggled and she had difficulty putting one foot in front of the other.

The few citizens out and about gazed in astonishment as she tottered down the middle of Main Street. She was almost opposite the law office when she suddenly collapsed.

Marshal Tim Ryan was the first person to reach her. The tall, lean lawman crouched down beside the fallen blonde, who had momentarily passed out. As a small crowd gathered, the marshal glanced up and instructed his deputy, young, redheaded Nick Pepper, to go fetch the doctor. But, before the deputy could depart, Audrey opened her eyes.

'No . . . no, I don't need no doctor,' she sighed, vainly attempting to rise.

With some assistance from Tim Ryan, she eventually managed to sit up. He gently supported her and asked, 'What in tarnation's happened to you, Miss Audrey?'

'Yes, *ma petite*, when you disappeared after the show last night, I assumed you were perhaps fatigued and had gone home to bed,' said a concerned Frenchie, who had pushed her way to the front of the small crowd to join the marshal.

'It . . . it's a long story,' said Audrey faintly.

'*Eh bien*, before you begin, let us get you indoors. You will be much more comfortable on the chaise longue in my sitting room,' declared the saloon keeper.

'Yeah, that's a darned good idea,' said Ryan.

Thereupon, he scooped the blonde up into his arms and, followed by Frenchie, Deputy Nick Pepper and the rest of the crowd, headed for the saloon.

Only the marshal, his deputy, Frenchie and Audrey passed through into the saloon-keeper's sitting room. The rest remained in the bar-room, where they stood around drinking and discussing what might have happened to the saloon-singer.

Meantime, in the privacy of Frenchie's sitting room, Audrey asked for a glass of water. Frenchie fetched a jug and poured Audrey a glassful. The blonde drained this thirstily and then held out the glass for a refill. The second glass she consumed rather less quickly and, when she had emptied it, Frenchie thrust a whiskey into her hand. Audrey slowly sipped the whiskey while she related her story.

She explained how the gambler, under the false name of Jerome Muggeridge, had tricked her into driving out with him into the desert, supposedly bound for Boulder City and an audition that could lead to the New York stage, and how he had abandoned her there. She quietly stated his reason for so doing. This brought forth an oath from the marshal, while her description of the discovery of the massacred Mexicans brought forth gasps of horror from all three of her listeners.

When she had finished, there followed a short silence. Marshal Tim Ryan was the first to speak.

'You said this feller, who drove you

out into the desert, called hisself Jerome Muggeridge, but that this wasn't his real name. Right?'

'He admitted as much,' replied Audrey.

'So, what *is* his real name?'

'I dunno.'

'But he's a pardner of Sam McClus-key?'

'I guess so.'

'To think that that goddam desperado spent the night here in Bonnie Springs! I could've nabbed the sonofabitch if only I'd known!'

'Never mind that, Marshal,' said Frenchie. 'What about those poor Mexican traders and their women lying dead out there in the desert, a prey to buzzards and coyotes?'

'They can wait.'

'But, Marshal . . . '

'First of all, me an' Nick gotta go look for their killers.'

'But where are you going to look, *mon ami*?'

'Why, right here in town. Yesterday, a

coupla what I took to be Mexican traders rode into town.'

'You think that they . . . ?'

'Could be the killers. Yeah, I do. Come on, Nick, let's git lookin'.'

The marshal and his young, red-headed deputy hurried from the room. Once the door had closed behind them, Frenchie turned to face Arizona Audrey.

'So, you were going to leave Frenchie's Place, *ma petite*?' she said reproachfully.

'I dunno, Frenchie. I was gonna audition. I thought it was my big chance, mebbe my only chance, to make the big time,' replied Audrey.

'I see.'

'But, of course, it turned out to be no chance at all.'

'No.'

'I wouldn't've jest vanished. I planned to come back an' tell you. Hell, I only had with me the clothes I stood up in!'

'Which are now in quite a state,' said Frenchie, with a wry smile.

'Yeah, they sure are!'

'OK, I suppose I would have done the same in your place,' remarked the saloon-keeper.

'You ain't mad at me, then?'

'No, Audrey, I am not. Come *ma chère*, what you need now is to get out of that dusty dress and into a nice, hot bath.'

'Oh, yes, please!' gasped Audrey.

A short while later, she was wallowing in a bath-tub, in a washroom at the rear of Frenchie's Place. And, at the same time, the marshal and his deputy were busily conducting their search for the Delgado brothers.

They discovered the mules, laden with blankets, abandoned in the livery stables and, shortly afterwards, found that the two Mexicans had spent the night at the Bonnie Springs Hotel. They also discovered that two other travellers, answering to the descriptions, given them by Arizona Audrey, of Sam McCluskey and Slim Jim Linn had shared a room at the hotel.

The outlaws had all signed the hotel register under false names. The Delgado brothers had used the name Lopez, while Sam McCluskey had signed in as Sam Smith and Slim Jim as James Brown.

'I take it these ain't their real names?' said Fred Gumbo, the manager of the Bonnie Springs Hotel.

'I don't think so,' said Ryan. 'Therefore, come, let's go verify they're who I think they are.'

'You figure you know all four, Marshal?' said his deputy.

'No, Nick, but I'm pretty certain I know three of 'em,' replied the marshal.

They thereupon retired to the law office, where Ryan dug out Wanted notices of Sam McCluskey, Luis Delgado and José Delgado. The ostler from the livery stables and both the manager of the Bonnie Springs Hotel and his porter identified the three outlaws. Of Slim Jim Linn, however, there was no Wanted poster and, consequently, he escaped identification.

'So,' mused Ryan, 'it would appear McCluskey an' this feller callin' hisself Muggeridge were here to rendezvous with the Delgado brothers.'

'Wa'al, certainly, they all four rode off together at first light,' said Fred Gumbo. 'Ain't that so, Jackie?'

'It sure is,' agreed the hotel porter.

'You saw 'em ride off?' rasped Tim Ryan.

'No, not exactly. We jest know they left the hotel then,' said Fred Gumbo. 'I was in the dinin' room an' Jackie was behind his desk when they all four came downstairs an' straight away went outside onto the stoop.'

'Yeah, an' a few minutes later, I heard the sound of horses' hoofs as they rode off down Main Street,' added the porter.

'So, do we ride out after 'em?' enquired Nick Pepper eagerly.

'We dunno where they're headed,' said Ryan, with a scowl. 'Nope. Guess now's the time to go fetch in the corpses of them poor murdered Mexicans. We'll go git Arizona Audrey to lead us to the spot where the massacre took place.'

They found Audrey back in Frenchie's sitting room, relaxed after her bath and with her feet cleansed, anointed with soothing oils and expertly bandaged by the Frenchwoman. The saloon-singer had dispensed with her stage gown and was wearing a fresh blue cotton dress that fell in full flare to her ankles. She was not at all keen to return to the scene of the massacre. However, Ryan pointed out that, if she didn't lead them there, it might take them some considerable time to find it. Consequently, the buzzards and coyotes could well leave them with darned little to bury. Accepting this, Audrey reluctantly agreed to act as their guide, and they went in search of Albert Boyd, the town mortician.

A few minutes later, a buckboard, driven by Boyd and with Audrey sitting up beside him, set forth flanked by the marshal and his deputy. Boyd had decided to use the buckboard, rather than his hearse, in view of the large number of corpses he was expecting to have to convey back into town.

They left behind them a town seething with curiosity. This was quickly satisfied by Fred Gumbo, his porter and the ostler, all three anxious to show off their knowledge. Soon, therefore, the entire community of Bonnie Springs was made aware that a quartet of desperate outlaws had stayed overnight at the hotel and that two of them had massacred a caravan of Mexican traders bound for Los Angeles. They waited in a state of high excitement for the return of Marshal Tim Ryan and his party.

Among the crowd awaiting the marshal's return were Jack Stone and Phineas Yeats. The Pinkerton detective had quizzed Fred Gumbo, the porter and the ostler at length and now he was anxious to question Arizona Audrey. And so, when he heard of the massacre, was Jack Stone.

He and Yeats had enjoyed the entertainment at Frenchie's Place and then, after a few beers, gone back to the hotel, intending to have an early night.

At breakfast they had discussed the wire which Yeats had received in reply to the one he had sent to Chicago. In it he had been instructed to await the arrival of another agent. The Pinkerton Detective Agency was not about to give up on its pursuit of Sam McCluskey, however cold the trail. But now everything was changed. Phineas Yeats could not afford to wait for the new agent, and Jack Stone, recalling his meeting with Pedro Fernandez and his friends, was determined to hunt down the ruthless men who had so callously murdered each and every one of the Mexican caravan.

It was mid-afternoon when Marshal Tim Ryan and his party rode back into Bonnie Springs, bringing with them the remains of the Mexicans. Albert Boyd headed for the funeral parlour with his buckboard and its grisly load, while the others made for Frenchie's Place. Ryan wanted Arizona Audrey to write and sign a statement, but firstly he, she and young Nick Pepper all badly needed a stiff whiskey.

They were besieged by a crowd of curious townsfolk, all eager to buy them a drink. But there was no need. Drinks were on the house.

Finally, when the colour had at last returned to Audrey's cheeks and they felt able to do what they had to do, they all three left the saloon and crossed the street to the law office. Nick Pepper closed the door behind them, shutting out the populace, and Tim Ryan sat Audrey down on his chair behind the desk. Thereupon, the blonde began to write out her statement.

It took her some time, but, eventually, both she and the marshal were satisfied with what she had written and she signed the statement.

She had scarcely done so when the law office door was pushed open and Phineas Yeats and Jack Stone stepped across the threshold.

'What the hell . . . ?' began Ryan.

'Sorry to interrupt,' said Yeats, 'but I got an interest here.'

'Oh, yeah?'

'Yeah. The name's Phineas Yeats an' I'm a Pinkerton man.' He offered the marshal his credentials and added, 'I'm on the trail of the outlaw, Sam McCluskey.'

'Is that so? An' your friend?'

'I wanta git the bastards who cut down those poor, defenceless traders. You could say this is personal.'

'You ain't a Pinkerton man, then?' said Ryan.

'Nope. Name's Jack Stone an' — '

'Jack Stone! The man who tamed Mallory?'

Stone smiled wryly. As usual, his reputation preceded him.

'Yup,' he said.

'You . . . you workin' on this case as a US marshal, Mr Stone?'

'Nope. Like I said, it's personal.'

'From what we've heard, McCluskey an' three others rendezvoused here in Bonnie Springs, then rode out at first light,' said Yeats.

'That's about it,' agreed Ryan.

'An' two of 'em carried out the

massacre of the Mexican traders?' said Stone.

'Yes, Mr Stone.'

'The young lady here discovered the bodies, I understand?'

'She did.'

'How come'?'

The marshal smiled encouragingly at the saloon-singer.

'Tell 'em, Miss Audrey,' he said.

Arizona Audrey took a deep breath and related the events of the previous evening, from her meeting with the mysterious Jerome Muggeridge up to the moment she stumbled across the corpses of the Mexican traders.

'It . . . it was horrible!' she concluded tearfully.

'Don't you take on, Miss Audrey,' said the marshal kindly. 'You're safe now an' among friends.'

'That's right, Arizona,' added Nick Pepper, using the blonde's stage name. 'You jest try 'n' put that goddam awful discovery behind you.'

For some moments the Kentuckian

and the Pinkerton detective mused upon what the girl had said. Then Stone spoke.

'The question is, why did Sam McCluskey, the Delgado brothers an' the feller callin' hisself Muggeridge choose to rendezvous here in Bonnie Springs?'

'I s'pose they could've been meetin' someone here?' suggested Yeats.

The marshal shook his head.

'I don't think so,' he said. 'Nobody else booked outa the hotel this mornin'. Fred Gumbo would've said if there'd been any more of 'em.'

'Any stranger ride into town this mornin' 'fore them varmints lit out?' asked Stone.

'Wa'al, yeah,' replied Ryan. 'A li'l ole white-haired, bespectacled feller in a black coat an' stovepipe hat rode in at first light. Looked like he'd be more at home in a pulpit than with McCluskey an' his gang. I figure we can discount him.'

Stone smiled at this description.

'Yeah, guess so,' he said.

'One thing's certain. They weren't aimin' to raid the bank here in town,' stated Yeats.

'No,' said Ryan.

'We know McCluskey was ridin' south, as were the Delgado brothers, for they ambushed that caravan some miles north of here,' said Yeats. 'S'pose Muggeridge was travellin' south too.'

'So what?' enquired Ryan.

'I reckon they rendezvoused here 'cause it was a convenient spot on their way south to wherever it is they plan to raid.'

'A bank?' said Ryan.

'Seems likely,' replied Yeats.

'But jest where?' muttered Stone.

'Flagstaff,' said Nick Pepper suddenly.

All the others turned their heads to stare at the young deputy.

'Why d'you say that, Nick?' asked Arizona Audrey.

''Cause this comin' Saturday Flagstaff holds its annual hoss fair, the biggest in the whole of the state of Arizona, 'deed the biggest 'tween El Paso an' 'Frisco. There'll be a whole heap of money in Flagstaff Saturday.'

'Dammit, you're right, Nick!' exclaimed the marshal. 'An' most of it'll be deposited for safe keepin' in the bank there. That's what them no-account critters are aimin' to raid!'

'We gotta stop 'em, Marshal,' said his deputy.

'But Flagstaff's way outa our jurisdiction. 'Sides, we gotta maintain law an' order hereabouts.'

'Don't worry. I'll go,' said Yeats.

'You cain't. Flagstaff's a two-hundred-mile ride from here,' said Stone.

'I'll make it,' stated Yeats.

'That wound of yourn — '

'Is fine. The doc bound it up real good. I'll make the ride easy.'

'Wa'al, I'm comin' with you.'

'This ain't your business, Jack.'

'As I said earlier, it's personal. Pedro Fernandez an' his people — '

'You hardly knew 'em.'

'That don't matter, Phineas. They was decent, law-abidin' folks, an' I aim to bring them murderin' Delgado brothers to book.'

'OK, Jack; if your mind's made up. Certainly, I'll be mighty glad of your company.'

'Then let's git goin',' said the Kentuckian, 'for they have a pretty good start on us, an' we wanta git there 'fore they raid that bank.'

'We sure as hell do!' agreed Yeats.

'Hang on a minute!' cried Ryan. 'Flagstaff's gonna be teemin' with folks from all over. The Delgados won't be the only Mexicans in town. You figure you can pick 'em out?'

'That could prove a mite tricky,' admitted the Pinkerton man.

'Yeah. An' while we got descriptions of McCluskey an' Muggeridge, we ain't never seen them either,' said Stone.

'Identifyin' the sonsofbitches ain't gonna be easy,' commented Ryan.

'No, I guess not,' said Yeats dolefully.

'But there *is* someone here who can

identify both Sam McCluskey an' the feller callin' hisself Muggeridge,' said the marshal.

All eyes turned to Arizona Audrey. She gasped and exclaimed, 'Oh, no, Marshal! Not me! I ain't goin' to Flagstaff nohow.'

'But you gotta, Arizona!' said Nick Pepper. 'If 'n you don't an' folks git killed . . .'

'But the show! I cain't jest up an' leave. Frenchie'll be madder'n a bear in a trap!'

'Wa'al, let's go see, shall we?' said Ryan.

In the event, Arizona Audrey was proved right. Frenchie was flaming mad, but not with the blonde. Having given Marshal Tim Ryan a piece of her mind, and told Jack Stone and Phineas Yeats to take good care of the blonde or they would have her to answer to, she turned to Audrey.

'Now, *ma petite*, do not take any risks. Be very, very careful. I want to see you back here safe and sound.'

'I'm so sorry, Frenchie. The show . . . '

'So we cancel a few performances. That is not what concerns me. It is for you that I worry, *mon amie*.'

The two women embraced and then, while Arizona Audrey changed into clothes suitable for the long ride, Stone went to the livery stables to pick out a horse for her. She admitted that she had ridden very little and, therefore, he found a gentle yet sound grey mare, which he felt would suit.

A few minutes later, the three set off, Phineas Yeats still nursing his shoulder wound and the saloon-singer clad in a grey, low-crowned, wide-brimmed Stetson, knee-length black leather jacket, check shirt, denim pants and soft buckskin boots, all provided out of town funds.

They rode in silence for the few miles to the Nevada-Arizona border. Then, as they crossed over, out of Nevada, the Kentuckian turned in the saddle and said, 'Guess you feel at home now, Arizona?'

'Why in tarnation should I?' retorted the blonde.

'Wa'al, you bein' back in your home state, of course.'

'This ain't my home state.'

'It ain't?'

Both Stone and Yeats looked non-plussed.

'No. I was born an' raised in Sacramento, California.'

'Then, why in blue blazes are you called Arizona Audrey?' demanded the Pinkerton man.

'That was Frenchie's idea,' she explained. 'Frenchie reckoned I needed a stage name an' she figured the name Arizona Audrey had a real good ring to it. Whaddya think?'

'I think we'll jest call you plain Audrey from now on,' said Stone.

And, with that, they once more rode on in silence.

6

When J. C. Sharkey and his gang rode into Flagstaff mid-way through Friday morning, the town was already teeming with people who had arrived early for Saturday's annual horse fair. There were ranchers, horse dealers, roustabouts, wranglers, mustangers, townsfolk, homesteaders, local Arapaho Indians, folks from the neighbouring states of California, Nevada, Utah, Colorado and New Mexico, and traders and vaqueros from Mexico itself.

Flagstaff was set to expand fourfold. Tents were going up all round the small town. Some big, some small. Saloons, bordellos, a boxing booth where Fighting Freddie Finlay's Professional Pugilists took on all-comers, a marquee containing the Seven Wonders of the World, including a bearded lady and the Strongest Man on Earth, stalls selling a variety of merchandise from ten-gallon hats to gaily-coloured rag dolls, and a host of multifarious establishments surrounded the town.

Itinerant medicine-men, fortune-tellers, card-sharps, jugglers, fire-eaters and assorted mountebanks poured in, all eager to ply their various trades.

Main Street hadn't been so crowded since Independence Day, the fourth of July. Now people were arriving all the time, on horseback, in buckboards, phaetons, gigs and covered wagons. J. C. Sharkey and his companions wended their way through the traffic until they reached the Bucking Bronco saloon. They hitched their horses to the rail outside, clattered up the half-dozen wooden steps to the stoop, pushed open the batwing doors and went inside.

The Bucking Bronco had a large bar-room, with a railed walkway which ran all the way round the saloon's upper level. This was reached by a staircase to one side of the bar, with its solid mahogany bar top. Although it was still morning, the bar-room was already fairly full. Half-a-dozen drinkers lined the bar, drinking and chatting to two of the saloon-girls. The rest of the saloon-girls were upstairs tending to the needs of their customers. In addition, several of the tables were occupied, and a mixture of townsfolk and homesteaders were playing poker at a table in the far corner of the saloon.

It had been a long, hot, dusty ride from Bonnie Springs. In consequence, all five were parched.

'Five beers,' said Sharkey to one of the Bucking Bronco's two bartenders.

The beer came up cold and frothy, and it went down the throats of Sharkey and the others in next to no time. All five sighed with satisfaction and slammed down their empty glasses onto the mahogany bar-top.

'Same again,' said Sharkey.

This time, when the beer came up, they took their glasses across to one of the few unoccupied tables. They sat down and, after checking that they were unlikely to be overheard, Sharkey addressed the others in a low voice.

'OK, boys,' he said, 'looks like we're here in good time.'

'So, what's our first move, J.C.?' enquired McCluskey.

'I figure you an' me'll mosey on over to the bank an' reconnoitre the situation,' replied Sharkey.

'An' what do we do?' asked Slim Jim Linn.

'You three stay put. We'll report back. OK?'

'It is OK by me,' said Luis Delgado, taking a large draught of the ice-cold beer and smiling widely.

'And me,' agreed his brother.

'Fine,' said Slim Jim.

Sharkey and McCluskey tossed back their beers, then rose and headed for the door. Outside, they joined the crowds bustling up and down Main Street.

The First National Bank stood some fifty or so yards down the busy thoroughfare and immediately opposite the law office. J. C. Sharkey scowled.

He would have preferred the two to be at opposite ends of Main Street. He carefully surveyed the bank as he and McCluskey walked slowly past. It was a one-storey, frame building with two large rectangular-shaped windows on either side of its entrance.

'OK,' he said, 'take a look round that there general store. I'm goin' into the bank. I'll come find you in the store when I'm finished.'

'But, J.C.,' protested McCluskey, 's'pose the storekeeper asks me what I'm lookin' for?'

'Wa'al, improvise, Sam. Tell him you wanta buy bullets for your gun or somethin',' said Sharkey testily, and he promptly turned on his heel and headed back towards the bank.

Once inside, Sharkey found four customers ahead of him. There was a grille along the length of the bank with two slots cut into it where the customers were being served. It seemed that the bank staff numbered only two, the manager and his clerk. While he waited his turn, Sharkey studied these two employees of the First National Bank.

The manager was a tall beanpole of a man. Silas Casson was in his mid-forties, thin-faced, thin-lipped and wan looking, with a lugubrious demeanour, a long nose and sombre grey eyes. He was dressed in an immaculate grey three-piece suit and tie. His clerk, Bob Garner, a spotty, short, flabby and bespectacled youth, was somewhat less grandly attired in a threadbare black jacket and trousers, well-worn white shirt and black bootlace tie.

When it came to his turn, Sharkey found himself confronting the bank manager. He smiled benignly.

'Good mornin'.'

''Morning, sir. How can I help you?' enquired Casson.

'I'm in town with some hosses to sell.'

'Yessir?'

'It could be I got me a whole heap of money come tomorrow evenin'.'

'I hope you are successful, sir.'

'Yeah. Wa'al, if'n I am, might I prevail upon your bank to hold that money for me?'

'You are not a customer of the First National?'

'Nope.'

'But you would like to deposit any profits you may make from the sale of your horses with us?'

'You got it.'

'That would be perfectly satisfactory, though you do understand that we would have to charge you a small fee?'

'That's OK.'

'And we could, of course, transfer the money to your own bank for another small fee.'

'I see.' Sharkey frowned slightly. 'I s'pose my money *would* be quite safe here?' he murmured.

'It would be kept in our safe.' Silas Casson indicated the huge steel box standing in the office behind him. 'Nobody's going to break into that,' he proclaimed proudly.

'There is a key?'

'Which I hold.'

'But if someone were to set upon you an' steal the key . . . '

'Usually I keep it on my person. However, as a precaution on the day of our horse fair, the bank holding so much more money than usual, I place it in the care of our sheriff. He retains the key until Monday morning when the bank's wagon, complete with armed escort, arrives in town to transfer the surplus money to our vaults in Los Angeles.'

Sharkey smiled. If Casson hadn't told him that, he would have deemed Slim Jim Linn and his safe-blowing skills surplus to requirements.

'Splendid!' he said. 'Then, if all goes well, I'll drop in tomorrow after the sales. What time does the bank close?'

'Usually six o'clock, but, on the day of the annual horse fair, we remain open till eight.'

'Thank you. Good day, Mr . . . er . . . ?'

'Casson.'

'Good day, Mr Casson.'

'Good day, sir.'

A smiling J. C. Sharkey left the bank and made his way along the sidewalk to the general store, where he found McCluskey pretending to be interested in the store's range of hats.

'OK, Sam, let's go,' he said.

Much relieved, the big outlaw followed Sharkey outside.

'Where to now?' he growled.

'We take a look out back,' said Sharkey.

They strolled slowly down the narrow alleyway between the bank and the general store. Normally, they would have found themselves confronted with a huge expanse of sagebrush desert, dotted here and there with mesquite, yucca and Joshua trees. But, on this occasion, they faced the boxing booth, one of the many tents being erected all round Flagstaff.

This suited Sharkey's purpose perfectly, for they could make out they were looking at the various stalls while, in fact, they were scrutinizing the rear of the bank. Again there was but the one door, on either side of which were two small, barred windows. The door itself looked extremely solid and the lock impossible to force without creating a great deal of noise. Sharkey assimilated all of this information as they walked past.

They turned into the next alley leading back to Main Street.

'You seen enough, J.C.?' enquired McCluskey.

'Yup.'

'So, it's back to the saloon?'

'Yup.'

'You figured out how we're gonna tackle this job?'

'I sure have.' Sharkey grinned. 'You observe that church we passed as we rode into town?' he asked.

'Yeah. A real neat frame buildin', painted white.'

'Did you read the time of the Sunday mornin' service as displayed on its notice board?'

‘Ten o’ clock, I b’lieve.’

‘That’s how I remember it. I’ll check, though, before we go into action.’

McCluskey looked baffled. What in tarnation, he wondered, had the time of the church service to do with their proposed bank raid? Before he could ask, they had reached the Bucking Bronco and Sharkey was pushing his way in through the batwing doors.

Moments later, they were reunited with Slim Jim Linn and the Delgado brothers. McCluskey and Slim Jim fetched a fresh round of beers for themselves and the Mexicans and a whiskey for Sharkey. Then, in a low voice, the little bank robber began.

‘It’s gonna be a piece of cake,’ he said.

‘You have now finalized your plans, J.C.?’ said Luis Delgado.

‘Yup.’

‘So, when do we raid the bank? Before or after it closes tomorrow?’ rasped McCluskey.

‘We don’t raid the bank tomorrow.’

'We don't?'

'No, Sam. We raid it at exactly five minutes past ten on Sunday morning. I'll explain.' Sharkey smiled slyly and continued, 'By then the tents and the crowds will have gone, Flagstaff will be back to normal, an' the citizens will all be in church attendin' the mornin' service. The perfect time for our raid. When Slim Jim blows the safe, the explosion will bring 'em runnin', but the church is on the very edge of town. We'll be ridin' hell-for-leather out the other end 'fore they can git halfway to the bank.'

'Why do we not strike during the hours of darkness, between midnight Saturday an' dawn Sunday?' asked Luis Delgado.

'My brother is right,' added José eagerly.

'Your brother is wrong,' stated Sharkey. 'Followin' the hoss fair, the high jinks are likely to go into the small hours. Which means the law'll still be up an' about. 'Sides, we need the key to the bank's back door.'

'I do not understand?' said Luis.

'Nor me,' added McCluskey, wrinkling his brow.

'Mr Casson, the bank manager, holds that key. He does not, however, hold the key to the safe. That, on the day of the hoss fair, is seemingly in the possession of the sheriff.'

'You're aimin' to take the back door key off this bank manager, J.C.?'

'Right, Sam. I figure we'll mosey on round his home an' — '

'You know where he lives?'

'Nope, but I intend to find out.'

'So, we go round an' take the key. Then what?'

'We bind an' gag him an' his family, assumin' he's got a family, then we head for the bank. Luis, you an' your brother will stay with the hosses. Sunday mornin' we'll take 'em an' hitch 'em outside this here saloon so as not to arouse any suspicions. When you hear the explosion as the safe blows, you bring the hosses along to the bank, pronto.'

'And what will you and Sam be doing?' enquired Luis.

'We'll be helpin' Slim Jim to stuff the contents of the safe into saddle-bags, ready for a real quick getaway.'

Sam McCluskey's ugly features split into a wide grin.

'I like it, J.C.!' he exclaimed.

The others murmured their approval.

'I don't s'pose anyone's likely to recognize us,' said Sharkey. 'But I reckon it's best if'n we split up. There's plenty to see an' do. There's boxin' to watch, sportin' women to tumble, whiskey to drink . . . '

'Only if you can afford it,' muttered Slim Jim.

'You broke?'

'Yes, J.C.'

'The rest of you?'

McLuskey and the Mexicans shook their heads. Sharkey smiled, produced a wad of banknotes and peeled off a few. He handed them to the gambler.

'That enough to keep you goin'?'

'Yeah. Gee, thanks, J.C.'

'I suggest we meet tomorrow at eight sharp for breakfast an' a run-through of our plan. There's a cantina a coupla doors down from the bank. Miguel's it's called. We'll rendezvous there.'

So saying, Sharkey threw back the remains of his whiskey and left the saloon. He intended finding a hotel room, where he planned to have a few hours' sleep. Then, he would grab something to eat and, when the bank closed, be ready to follow the manager to his home. Once he knew where Casson lived, he could relax and enjoy himself. He smiled quietly. Although he was no longer in the first flush of youth, J. C. Sharkey still had lead in his pencil, and there was a certain redhead he had spotted in the Bucking Bronco Saloon . . .

7

There was, as J. C. Sharkey had said, plenty to see and do in Flagstaff that Friday evening. But, as far as Slim Jim Linn was concerned, there was only one thing he *wanted* to do. He wanted to play poker. Which is how he came to be sitting in the vast, ornate bar-room of the Alhambra Hotel that evening when Arizona Audrey, Jack Stone and Phineas Yeats entered through its portals.

All three were dusty, tired and travel-stained. Audrey's feet, although encased in soft buckskin, still hurt pretty badly. And now, in addition, her buttocks were saddle-sore. Consequently, she declined the Kentuckian's suggestion that they should sit down and have a drink.

'A drink'll be fine, for I'm as dry as that goddam desert out there. But I ain't sittin',' she stated flatly.

Stone grinned and ordered three beers. Ordinarily, the blonde would have had a whiskey. Beer was not a drink she favoured. However, in her present parched condition, she needed a drink that was both long and cold.

'That's better,' she murmured, as the beer hit the spot.

'So, what now?' said Phineas Yeats.

'Three things,' replied Stone. 'We book ourselves into this here hotel, we git a doctor to take a look at your wound an' then we find somethin' to eat.'

'I noticed a dinin'-room on the other side of the lobby as we came in,' said Yeats.

'That'll do us fine.'

'Not me, it won't!' declared Audrey.

'No?'

'No, Jack. You can bring somethin' up to my room. I'll eat it standin' up.'

Again Stone grinned, while Yeats laughed outright.

'It ain't funny,' said Audrey.

The two men straightened their faces and, when presently all three had finished their beers, they returned to the lobby. The clerk behind the reception desk had them sign the register, then showed them upstairs to their three separate rooms. He promised to fetch a doctor to tend to Yeats' wound.

Meantime, downstairs in the barroom, Slim Jim Linn was not a happy man, for he had imagined he would never ever see Arizona Audrey again. What in blue blazes, he asked himself, was she doing in Flagstaff? And who the hell were her companions? He thanked his lucky stars that she had not glanced in the direction of the poker table. Had she done so, she would have almost certainly spotted him.

Slim Jim had not overheard the conversation at the bar, but he wondered whether Audrey and the two men might possibly be staying at the Alhambra. He determined to check, but later when it was likely they would have retired to their beds. He had no wish to confront the blonde while she was with her friends, who, Slim Jim suspected, could well be peace officers. If she were on his trail, as he rather thought she might be, he was in a tough spot. Her presence in Flagstaff put J. C. Sharkey's plans in jeopardy. So, what should he do? For the moment, he decided to try to concentrate on his poker-playing.

The evening progressed. Doc Carter, small, rotund, red-faced and bespectacled, called at the hotel and dressed and bandaged Phineas Yeats' wound. He pronounced that, while it was healing reasonably well, it would heal quicker if the Pinkerton man did nothing strenuous. His horse-ride from Bonnie Springs had not helped. The doctor said he would call again in a day or two to check it and, if necessary, change the dressing.

Immediately thereafter, Yeats and the Kentuckian made their way downstairs to the dining-room, where they ate a hearty supper. Then, Yeats announced that he intended retiring early. Stone said he would take Arizona Audrey something to eat and then probably have a few whiskies in the bar-room before he, too, retired for the night.

Some minutes later, Stone tapped on Audrey's door. He was bearing a plate of tacos filled with minced beef chilli.

'Come in,' cried the blonde.

Stone stepped into the bedroom and almost dropped the plate, for Audrey was sitting up in bed and was stark naked. He gazed lustfully at the blonde's small, firm breasts peeking out from above the bedclothes, and felt more than just his temperature begin to rise.

'Holy cow!' he exclaimed.

Arizona Audrey smiled seductively.

'You like what you see, Jack?'

'Er . . . yeah, you're darned tootin' I do!'

'Then, why don't you join me?'

'What . . . what about your supper?'

'I think that can wait till later. Don't you?'

'Yup.'

The Kentuckian grinned. He and Yeats had got onto first name terms with the saloon-singer during their long ride across the desert. And they had spent three nights under the stars, but quite innocently. Therefore, the blonde's invitation had taken him by surprise. He put down the plate, hung his Stetson, gun-belt, holster and gun on one of the bedposts and proceeded to undress hurriedly.

'One thing, though, Jack,' said Audrey.

'Yeah?'

'My ass bein' so darned sore, it's gotta be me on top.'

Again the Kentuckian grinned.

'We'll do it any way you like,' he replied eagerly, and, stepping out of his denim pants, he leapt into bed and pulled the blonde into his arms.

While Stone and the saloon-singer were making love upstairs, Slim Jim Linn continued to play poker downstairs. Lady Luck was favouring him with the right cards and, although he was finding it difficult to concentrate, he did reasonably well. He was an experienced and skilful card-player and more than a match for the others round the table. Had it not been for his preoccupation regarding Arizona Audrey's sudden and unforeseen appearance in town, he would undoubtedly have made a real killing. As it was, when he left the table at midnight, Slim Jim had at least made a tidy profit.

He found the hotel lobby deserted. The register lay open on top of the reception desk. Slim Jim turned it round and studied it. Arizona Audrey was in room number fourteen. The gambler hesitated. What should he do? Finally, he made up his mind. He would visit the blonde and demand to know what she was doing in town. Once he had her answer, he would determine what to do next.

Softly, cautiously, he climbed the stairs. The corridor, on each side of which stood the bedrooms, was dimly lit by a couple of brass lamps, one at either end. Slim Jim made his way slowly along this corridor, peering at each door number in turn. Eventually, he found himself standing before number fourteen. He tried the handle. It turned and, as he pushed, the door swung open. Unfortunately, the hinges badly needed oiling and it creaked.

Jack Stone immediately sat up. Their hectic lovemaking concluded, Arizona Audrey, tired out by that and by her long day in the saddle, had promptly fallen asleep. Stone, however, remained awake. He was happily contemplating another session with the blonde in the morning when the sound of the door creaking open roused him from his torpor. He grabbed the Frontier Model Colt out of the holster hanging on the bedpost and, as Slim Jim popped his head round the door, loosed off a quick shot.

Slim Jim's luck held. The Kentuckian's shot was hurried and the bullet ripped into the door an inch above the gambler's head, sending splinters flying in all directions. By the time Stone fired a second time, the door had slammed shut and Slim Jim was halfway down the corridor towards the stairs.

Arizona Audrey, meantime, had also shot bolt upright in bed.

'What . . . what the heck's goin' on?' she demanded.

'Someone tried to sneak into our room. A thief, I guess,' said Stone as, still clutching the revolver, he covered the distance between the bed and the door in three long strides.

He pulled open the door.

'You cain't go after him, Jack!' cried Audrey. 'Goddammit, you're stark naked!'

Stone's two shots had wakened several of the other guests in the hotel and they, too, appeared in their doorways in various states of undress. Phineas Yeats, wearing only the bandage with which Doc Carter had bound his wound, spoke for all of them.

'I heard shootin',' he said. Glancing at the gun in the Kentuckian's hand, he asked, 'Who, in tarnation, you been firin' at?'

'Some goddam thief who tried to sneak into my bedroom,' replied Stone.

Yeats grinned.

'*Your* bedroom?'

Stone grinned back.

'Me an' Audrey, we figured it'd be more fun to share a bed than sleep on our own.'

'Yeah, wa'al, whaddya gonna do 'bout the thief?'

'Nuthin'.'

'Nuthin'?'

'Nope. I cain't see him comin' back. An' there ain't no point chasin' after him. By the time I git dressed — '

'Quite so.' Yeats regarded Stone with an ironical eye. 'Good night, then, Jack.' And in a louder voice: 'Good night, Audrey!'

Stone closed the door and headed towards the bed. He replaced the Frontier Model Colt in its holster and climbed back in beside the blonde.

'That li'l incident's sure woken me

up,' he said. ''Deed, I don't feel the least bit like sleepin'. Not yet awhiles, anyway.'

'I'll git back on top, then, Jack,' said Audrey, with an impish grin.

Meanwhile, unaware that no pursuit was likely and completely unnerved by the two shots aimed at him, Slim Jim Linn had run pell-mell from the hotel and out into Main street.

Now, while the Alhambra's guests were once more settling down for the night, he hared down the sidewalk, desperately looking for somewhere to hide. Ahead of him a red light glistened: the Cactus Flower, usually Flagstaff's one and only bordello. Slim Jim dived inside.

Like most of the premises along Main Street, the Cactus Flower was a two-storey frame building. Downstairs consisted of one large room, where the bordello's customers chatted to, and ran their eyes over, the sporting women before disappearing upstairs to one of the bedrooms with the woman of their choice.

The lights were dimmed and the air heavy with perfume. Red velvet predominated. At one corner was a small bar behind which the madame dispensed drinks. She smiled contentedly, for the influx of visitors attending the Flagstaff horse fair had provided her establishment with more than a few extra customers.

Slim Jim Linn glanced round anxiously and then made a grab for one of the few women not being propositioned, a large, plump brunette with breasts the size of watermelons. He was keen to be hidden away in one of the upstairs bedrooms before any pursuer chanced to stick his head through the bordello's door. Consequently, he dispensed with the usual formalities and, instead, straightway made for the stairs with the brunette in tow. He had only just reached their foot when the madame intervened.

'This establishment requires that payment should be made in advance,' she informed him.

'How much?' he enquired.

The madame looked him over and, observing that he was in one heck of a hurry to hustle the brunette upstairs, demanded twice the usual rate. Slim Jim paid up without a murmur and continued on his way.

'That's what I like,' commented the madame, 'a feller who knows his mind.'

8

Slim Jim Linn sighed. Since parting from the brunette, he had been seriously considering his options in the light of Arizona Audrey's recent arrival in town. And he had come to the conclusion that it would be best to simply skedaddle and leave J. C. Sharkey and his pals to conduct their bank raid without him. Unfortunately, however, he had run into the Delgado brothers as he headed for the livery stables. Consequently, he now had no choice other than to proceed to the rendezvous at Miguel's.

On reaching the restaurant, they found J. C. Sharkey and Sam McCluskey seated at a table by the window, smoking cigars and drinking coffee.

Sharkey consulted his gold hunter.

'Eight o'clock,' he pronounced. 'I'm glad to see you boys is punctual.'

He smiled and summoned a waitress. They thereupon ordered breakfast.

Once this had been served and the waitress departed, Sam McCluskey asked quietly, 'Did you find out where the bank manager lives, J.C.?'

'Sure did, Sam. Won't he be surprised when we pay him a call tomorrow mornin'?'

'We had best go early,' said Luis Delgado. 'We need to catch him before he goes to church.'

'Yeah. We'll meet here at nine. Then, like I said, we take care of the bank manager an' git hold of the key to the bank's back door. After that, we do exactly as I told you yesterday. Slim Jim'll fix to blow the safe at precisely five minutes past ten. By then the good folk of Flagstaff should be at prayer. I figure we'll have completed our business 'fore they can git up off their knees.'

'That's right, J.C. We'll have the money an' be outa town 'fore you can say Jack Robinson!' chortled McCluskey.

‘Wa’al, that’s the plan,’ said Sharkey. He looked round the others. ‘Any comments?’ he asked.

‘No. I like your plan,’ said Luis, adding, with a gleam in his eye, ‘If anyone does try to stop us, José and I will kill them.’

‘*Sí*, J.C.,’ affirmed José.

‘That’s why I invited you boys along,’ said Sharkey. He turned to face Slim Jim. ‘Fixin’ to blow the safe at precisely five minutes past ten won’t pose no problem, will it?’

‘Er . . . no . . . no, ’course not,’ lied the gambler. Then, summoning up his courage, he blurted out, ‘But we *do* have a problem.’

Sharkey fixed Slim Jim Linn with a hard, penetrating stare.

‘Explain,’ he said quietly.

‘It’s ’bout that saloon-singer back in Bonnie Springs, Arizona Audrey.’

‘Yes?’

‘You know I was given the task of inveiglin’ her out into the desert an’ killin’ her?’

'An' that's exactly what you did,' interjected McCluskey.

'Not *exactly*,' said Slim Jim.

'But you said . . .'

'I jest couldn't bring myself to shoot her, Sam. I left her out there, figurin' that, by the time she made it back to town, we'd all be long gone.'

'OK, so you didn't kill her. So what?' demanded Sharkey.

'She . . . she's here in Flagstaff.'

'What!' McCluskey stretched across the table and grabbed the gambler by the throat. 'You goddamn, yeller-livered little sonofabitch, I'll have your guts for — '

'Take it easy, Sam,' said Sharkey, intervening and pulling the big outlaw back into his seat.

McCluskey reluctantly released his grip on Slim Jim's throat and the gambler collapsed on to his chair, gasping for breath.

'I . . . I'm sorry, Sam,' he said. 'I simply couldn't do it. An' I never, for one moment, expected her to turn up here.'

'No, I guess not. The question is, what is she doin' here?' mused Sharkey.

'I dunno. Could be a coincidence.'

'I don't believe in coincidences. Where'd you see her, Slim Jim?'

'In the Alhambra Hotel, in company with two fellers.'

'Oh, yeah?'

'Yeah. I checked the register. They're all three of 'em stayin' there.'

'You remember the names of her companions?'

'I sure do, J.C. They signed theirselves in as J. Stone an' P. Yeats.'

'Holy cow!' exclaimed McCluskey.

Sharkey smiled thinly.

'Like me, you recognize the name, Stone?'

'I do.'

'Jack Stone. He's somethin' of a legend in the West.'

'A lawman?' enquired Slim Jim nervously.

'That's how he earned his formidable reputation. But I'd heard he'd retired.'

'Me, too,' confirmed McCluskey.

'What about the other feller?' said Slim Jim.

'His name don't ring no bells with me. Does it with any of you?' Sharkey enquired of the others.

'Nope,' said McCluskey.

The two brothers merely shook their heads.

'Describe him,' said Sharkey.

The gambler thought hard for a few moments, then gave as detailed a description as he could manage.

'Hmm. Wa'al, he ain't no cowpoke, that's for sure,' said McCluskey.

'No. My guess is he's a US marshal or some other kinda law enforcement officer,' said Sharkey.

'They're lookin' for us, ain't they?' remarked McCluskey.

'Possibly.'

'Probably.'

'OK, Sam. Probably.'

'So, what are we gonna do?'

'You four all stayed overnight in Bonnie Springs?'

'You know we did.'

'At the same hotel. Therefore, it's almost certain they're lookin' for a gang of four would-be bank robbers. They must've guessed that's why we're here.' Sharkey smiled coldly. 'It's unlikely they know about me.'

'No. An' I reckon the reason Stone an' his pardner have brought Arizona Audrey along is 'cause she's the only one can recognize us. Me an' Slim Jim, that is. I don't s'pose she ever saw Luis an' José.'

'I agree, Sam.'

'So, if we eliminate Arizona Audrey — '

'Goddammit, there she is!' exclaimed Slim Jim, staring out of the window at the three people crossing Main Street.

Jack Stone, Phineas Yeats and Arizona Audrey were on their way to the law office, which stood on the other side of Main Street. As they disappeared inside, Sharkey turned to the others.

'Killin' her here in town would not be a good idea,' he said.

'But she *is* here in town!' protested McCluskey.

'Then we gotta git her outa town. Like last time.'

'But how in tarnation do we do that, J.C.?'

'Shuddup for a second an' let me think.'

For the next few minutes, all that could be heard at their table was the slurping of coffee and the chomping of bacon, eggs and corn fritters, as McCluskey, Slim Jim and the Delgado brothers ate their breakfast and Sharkey gave the matter at hand some serious thought.

Finally, Sharkey looked up and smiled.

'You gotta plan?' enquired McCluskey hopefully.

''Deed I have,' said Sharkey, and he proceeded to outline it to the expectant gang. When he had finished, there was a short silence.

'Wa'al, whaddya think?' he snapped.

'It could jest work,' said Slim Jim.

'Sure it could,' said McCluskey. 'An' once we've got Arizona Audrey an' her two companions outa town an' headin' for — '

Sharkey interrupted him. 'You, Sam, will ride after 'em an' make darned sure they don't return.'

'But why would they? Surely there ain't no need to kill 'em?' protested Slim Jim.

'That's what you thought last time,' said Sharkey. 'This time I ain't takin' no chances.'

'OK. But if'n I ride after 'em an' do as you say, the chances are I won't git back to Flagstaff in time to join in your bank raid,' said McCluskey. 'I mean, I can hardly kill 'em in front of witnesses, an' there'll be folks still headin' here for the hoss fair. Which means that — '

'I figure we can manage without you.'

'But . . . '

'Don't worry, Sam. You'll git your share.'

'How?'

'After the raid we'll head for Providence Flats. I'll met you there at the Golden Garter an' settle up.'

'I dunno 'bout that. I . . .'

'Sam, I ain't gonna doublecross you. Hell, I don't fancy lookin' over my shoulder for the rest of my life!'

'Guess not, J.C.'

'Definitely not. An' Sam, a word of advice. Git yourself a Sharps rifle an' pick off Stone an' his pardner at long range. You can deal with the girl afterwards.'

'Right.'

Sharkey finished his coffee and stood up.

'I'll git started, then,' he said. 'Sam, you go git that there rifle. Luis, you be ready to follow Arizona Audrey an' her pals if'n they leave the law office before I return. They're gonna be out lookin' for Sam an' Slim Jim, but, sooner or later, they'll surely stop off for a drink or somethin' to eat. Then you high-tail it back here an' report. OK?'

'*Sí*, J.C.'

'What about me an' José?' enquired Slim Jim.

'You two ain't needed to do nuthin'.

You best stay here, though, till Arizona Audrey's safely outa town.'

'OK.'

Sharkey's scheme was a simple one, but it entailed employing an outsider, someone unaware of Sharkey's identity or his plan to rob the First National Bank. And that someone had to be an actor. Consequently, Sharkey left Miguel's and headed northwards along Main Street towards Flagstaff's Playhouse.

Nathaniel Peabody was the owner, manager, director, leading actor and resident playwright of the Playhouse. Sharkey found him directing a rehearsal for his latest creation, 'The Prince and the Orphan Girl', to be performed that very evening. Peabody was a large man in his early forties, rather corpulent and extremely flamboyant, with a plump red face, piggy black eyes and a splendidly curled jet-black moustache. He wore a brown Derby at a rakish angle, a bottle-green frock coat over a bright yellow brocade vest, and cream-coloured trousers tucked into shiny black boots. And he clutched a gold-topped cane.

Sharkey arrived inside the auditorium at an opportune moment, for Peabody had just announced to the cast that it was time for a short break. The actor-manager lit a large cigar and watched Sharkey make his way down the centre aisle towards the stage.

'Can I help you, sir?' he enquired in a loud, booming voice.

'Indeed you can,' said Sharkey. 'I assume you are in charge here?'

'I am. Nathaniel Peabody at your service.' So saying, the thespian gave Sharkey a courtly bow. 'And you are . . . ?' he said, as he straightened up.

'Smithers, J. C. Smithers,' replied Sharkey, adding without preamble, 'I should like to borrow one of your actors for an hour or so.'

'Ah! Now that could prove difficult. As you can see, my dear sir, we are busy rehearsing for tonight's performance.'

'I don't require a leading actor. One of your . . . er . . . minor players would do.'

'Wa'al . . . '

'As I said, it's only for an hour or so. I need him to help me play a jape on some friends of mine.'

'Wa'al . . . '

'I am happy to pay for his services.'

'Indeed?' The actor-manager's eyes lit up and he asked, 'How much?'

Sharkey produced a wad of dollar bills and peeled off ten. He offered them to Peabody.

'It'll be good practice for your actor,' he said, 'for he'll need to learn a few lines.'

Peabody hesitated while he calculated whether he could screw any more money out of this elderly, bespectacled stranger. The look in J. C. Sharkey's cold grey eyes told him that he couldn't.

'Very well,' he said. 'I believe I can spare you one of the younger members of my company, Mr Donny Evans.'

And so the matter was settled.

Donny Evans turned out to be an amiable, though rather gangly-looking, young man. New to the company and anxious to please the actor-manager, he was only too willing to place his acting talents at J. C. Sharkey's disposal for an hour or so, particularly as his role in 'The Prince and the Orphan Girl' could in no way be described as onerous.

He readily accepted Sharkey's explanation that he was simply taking part in a jape, and did not seem at all bothered that there was no written script. He and Sharkey rehearsed together for about half-an-hour and then they left the theatre and headed back towards Miguel's restaurant.

Meanwhile, Arizona Audrey, Jack Stone and Phineas Yeats were closeted in the law office with Sheriff John Baldwin, a lean, serious-faced man in his late thirties, and two of his deputies. Audrey told her story, the matter was thoroughly discussed and Wanted posters were closely studied.

Finally, Sheriff John Baldwin declared, 'Wa'al, folks, it seems to me that we got little or no chance of pickin' out the

Delgado brothers from the rest of the Mexicans attendin' our hoss fair.'

'That's right,' averred Stone. 'The only two we got any hope of identifyin' are Sam McCluskey an' the feller callin' hisself Jerome Muggeridge. If'n Audrey can spot 'em 'fore they try their hand at robbin' the bank, we can mebbe surprise an' capture 'em without no shoot-out.'

'You're sure that's what they're aimin' to do, rob the bank?' said Baldwin.

'It's gotta be, hasn't it?' said Yeats.

'Yeah, I guess so. If I was plannin' to rob it, this is the one day in the year I'd choose,' stated the sheriff.

'So, me an' Phineas an' Audrey, we'll search the town an', if an' when we find 'em, we'll report back,' said the Kentuckian. 'Then we can figure what to do, bearin' in mind that we also wanta arrest them two murderin' Mexicans.'

'OK,' said Baldwin. 'Me an' my deppities'll be ready an' waitin'.'

'Let's git goin', then,' said Stone.

'Yeah, let's,' agreed Phineas Yeats eagerly.

Arizona Audrey was not so keen. She wished it were all over, for she had no wish to confront either Sam McCluskey or her mysterious abductor, the man calling himself Jerome Muggeridge. Rather, she longed to be back on stage in Frenchie's Place, doing what she did best.

By coincidence, Stone and the others' visit to the law office had been of approximately the same duration as the time spent by J. C. Sharkey recruiting the services of, and rehearsing with, the young actor, Donny Evans. Consequently, Luis Delgado was not required to track the Kentuckian and his companions through the town. Pausing only to tell Sam McCluskey to remain in the restaurant until his return, Sharkey set off after them, accompanied by his new ally. McCluskey glowered. The prospect of being confined for some considerable time in Miguel's, and being obliged, as a result, to down further copious cups of coffee, did not appeal to the big outlaw. He glared angrily across the table at the gambler.

'This is all your fault, Slim Jim,' he growled. 'If'n you'd shot that goddam saloon-singer like I'd told you to, I could be out an' about, enjoyin' the hoss fair. Wa'al, I don't intend bein' stuck here on my lonesome. Luis an' José are free to go, but you're gonna stay an' keep me company.'

'My . . . my pleasure, Sam,' replied Slim Jim, nervously eyeing the newly-acquired Sharps rifle, which McCluskey was sitting clutching.

While McCluskey was venting his feelings, J. C. Sharkey was proceeding slowly through the throngs crowding Flagstaff's Main Street. Ahead of him, Arizona Audrey was anxiously scanning those same throngs in the vain hope of spotting either McCluskey, or Linn, or both.

She and her two companions progressed from the town to the tented village surrounding it. They visited each and every stall and sideshow, taking in, among others, the boxing booth and the Seven Wonders of the World. By noon, all three were hot and weary. As well as still being saddle-sore, Audrey was once again foot-sore, while Phineas Yeats' wound was paining him. Both were relieved when Stone suggested that they suspend their search for half-an-hour and refresh themselves at the Bucking Bronco. Their pace quickened as they headed from the tented village to the saloon.

Sharkey gave them sufficient time to order their first drink, then peered cautiously over the top of the batwing doors. He quickly observed that they were standing at the bar. He turned to Donny Evans.

'Wa'al, my boy, are you ready?' he enquired.

'Yessir,' replied the young actor.

'You can remember them lines I taught you?'

'Yessir.'

'Then, let our play-actin' begin.'

So saying, Sharkey thrust against the door, stepped inside and made his way in leisurely fashion across the bar-room towards the mahogany-topped bar.

As he approached the three drinkers, he turned to his companion, winked and commenced speaking in a voice loud enough for Stone and the others to hear: 'I dunno who the rest were, a coupla Mexicans an' some other feller, but their leader was apparently the notorious outlaw, Sam McCluskey.'

'An' they were all captured as they stepped into the bank?' said Donny Evans.

''S'right. McCluskey had been spotted an' recognized earlier in the day. The sheriff guessed they intended raidin' the bank an' he set a trap for 'em.'

'Holy cow!'

'Unfortunately, he was kinda too quick on the draw.'

'Whaddya mean?'

'Wa'al, they hadn't actually stuck up

the bank when he an' his deppities jumped 'em.'

'No?'

'No. They claim they had no intention of doin' so, an', into the bargain, McCluskey claims he ain't McCluskey.'

'So, what happens now?'

'It's jest this one guy who recognized McCluskey. So, it's his word against McCluskey's.' Sharkey paused and added, 'McCluskey's got some hot-shot lawyer actin' for him who's screamin' habeas corpus. If'n the sheriff don't soon come up with someone else who can identify McCluskey, I reckon he'll have to let all four of 'em go.'

'No!'

'I'm afraid so.'

It was at this juncture that Jack Stone intervened. He put down his glass of beer, turned and addressed Sharkey.

'Excuse me, mister,' he said. 'I couldn't help but overhear your conversation.'

'So?' said Sharkey.

'So, tell me, whereabouts were Sam McCluskey an' his pardners arrested?'

'In Kingman.'

'When was this?'

'Three days back. I would've liked to stay an' see the sonsofbitches hang, but I have important business to transact at the hoss fair.'

'I see.'

''Sides, there won't be no hangin' unless the sheriff finds a second witness to verify McCluskey's identity.'

'How long d'you figure he's got before that lawyer you mentioned gits McCluskey released?'

'Dunno for sure. But I'd say days rather than weeks.'

'OK. Thanks, mister.'

Sharkey nodded, then steered the young actor to the far end of the bar, where he ordered a couple of beers. The play-acting was over.

'You said, when you hired me, that this was part of a jape you were playin' on your friends,' said Donny Evans.

'Correct.'

'But you didn't seem to know those folks. Leastways . . . '

'Did I say *my* friends?'

'You did.'

'Wa'al, I meant friends of a friend. I'm simply obligin' a third party.'

'Oh, I see!'

Sharkey smiled and patted his companion on the shoulder. He glanced along the bar and was gratified to observe Stone, Yeats and the blonde deep in conversation. He had no doubt whatsoever that, within the next half-hour, they would all three be riding across the desert towards the distant town of Kingman.

'Kingman!' exclaimed Stone. 'Why in tarnation did they choose to raid the bank in Kingman? 'Tain't no bigger than Flagstaff an' there ain't no hoss fair takin' place there.'

'No.' Yeats scratched his head. 'It don't make no sense, but seems that's what they've gone an' done.'

'Mebbe they didn't know 'bout the hoss fair,' suggested Audrey.

'Guess that must be the answer. Anyways, if Sam McCluskey ain't to git clean away, you'll have to go an' identify him,' said the Kentuckian.

'Me? Hell, Jack, surely someone nearer at hand'll come forward? Kingman's gotta be at least a hundred miles from here.'

'One hundred an' thirty.'

'Oh, no!'

'Unfortunately, we don't know for sure that someone else will turn up an' identify him,' stated Yeats.

'Phineas is right. You ain't got no choice, Audrey, you gotta go.' Stone smiled gently. 'Don't worry, I'll ride with you,' he said.

'Me, too,' said Yeats.

Stone glanced anxiously at the Pinkerton detective.

'You sure, Phineas?' he asked. 'That wound of yourn . . . '

'Is a lot better.' Yeats looked the other straight in the eye and stated, 'I'm ridin' along, an' that's final.'

'OK.'

'Wa'al, before we set out, I'm goin' shoppin',' declared Audrey.

'Shoppin'! What the heck are you aimin' to buy?' cried Stone.

'My ass is still pretty darned tender. I'm gonna git me a cushion.'

Stone laughed.

'OK,' he said. 'Only don't be too long about it. We ain't got much time to spare.'

In the event, all three were in the saddle within twenty minutes of leaving the Bucking Bronco. A brand-new red satin cushion decorated Arizona Audrey's saddle and happily the blonde found the contact between it and her bottom rather less painful than she had feared. They rode across the town limits and then turned westwards towards Kingman.

Sam McCluskey gave Arizona Audrey and her two companions a good start. Firstly, he had no wish that they should spot him and, secondly, he dared not shoot them until the trail was completely deserted, for he wanted no witnesses to the three murders he proposed to commit.

The afternoon wore on and, as it did so, the number of people travelling towards Flagstaff diminished. Presently, the trail emptied, but by now McCluskey's quarry were no longer riding across the vast, open expanse of desert. Instead, they were following the trail as it wound its way through wooded hilly country beneath and beyond Humphrey's Peak and running parallel to the Grand Canyon.

The outlaw cursed loud and long. Had the trail emptied earlier, he could easily have picked off all three. Now the twists and turns of the trail effectively hid them from view. He spurred his horse on. Eventually, they would again emerge on to the desolate desert, where they should provide easy targets, but that would not be until morning. By then it would be too late for him to make the return journey to Flagstaff in time to participate in Sharkey's bank raid.

Ahead of him, his quarry pressed

forward relentlessly. Jack Stone was anxious that they should reach Kingman with all possible speed, since he was afraid McCluskey might be released before they got there. In consequence, he kept urging the others on. They, for their part, were both flagging. Audrey grew wearier and wearier with each passing mile, while Yeats' wound was undoubtedly taking its toll. Nevertheless, they rode on through the evening until, shortly after ten o'clock, the blonde finally cried halt.

'I cain't ride no further!' she sighed. 'I need a rest an' somethin' to eat an' drink.'

'Yeah. Let's take a breather,' concurred Yeats.

'OK,' said Stone. 'We'll do jest that. I guess there ain't no way we can ride the whole way to Kingman without stoppin'.'

Although it was dark, they were able to see well enough, by the light of the stars, to build a small camp-fire and brew some coffee. The spot they had chosen was just off the main trail, in a large hollow with hills on three sides.

Sam McCluskey was half-a-mile back when he spotted the firelight. He smiled grimly and reined in his horse. Then, pulling the Sharps rifle from the saddleboot, he dismounted, tethered the horse to a nearby cottonwood tree and began to clamber up the hillside to his left. The hill was a low one and it took him only a few minutes to reach its summit.

From this vantage point, McCluskey overlooked his quarry's camp. At no more than a half-mile's distance, they were within easy range of his long-barrelled buffalo gun. The big outlaw crouched down and rested the Sharps' long barrel on top of the boulder in front of him. He began to focus on the three figures sitting huddled round the camp-fire. Sharkey's advice promptly sprang to mind. He was to take out the two men first. McCluskey adjusted his aim slightly. Now it was Phineas Yeats' figure which came sharply into focus.

McCluskey curled his finger round the trigger of the Sharps rifle. Then he slowly squeezed it.

The report sounded louder than usual as it broke the silence of the night. It was followed instantly by Yeats' cry. The Pinkerton man was struck in the back of the skull, and he pitched forward across the camp-fire. In so doing, his body collapsed on to the fire, temporarily extinguishing the flames and plunging the hollow into darkness.

This all happened so quickly that McCluskey was unable to focus on the Kentuckian before he and the blonde were swallowed up by the darkness into which their stricken companion had plunged them. The outlaw cursed and peered anxiously into the hollow. As the sparks vanished into the sky, his night-vision adjusted itself. Although the light from the fire was no longer available to him, there remained the starlight and this should have been sufficient for him to make out the dark shapes of Stone and the girl. But there was no sign of either of them. The hollow lay dark and empty. Where in tarnation were they, he asked himself angrily?

The answer was simple. Unbeknown to the outlaw, an arroyo cut through the hollow. In midwinter this watercourse sometimes had a trickle running through, but not in October. In the instant that Phineas Yeats had been hit and pitched forward on to the fire, Jack Stone had grabbed Arizona Audrey and thrown both her and himself into the arroyo. While Sam McCluskey vainly ran his gaze over the floor of the hollow, Stone and the blonde remained hidden beneath the rim of the dried-up watercourse. Even in broad daylight it would have been difficult, at a distance of half-a-mile, to pick out the arroyo. In the darkness, it was quite impossible.

'What the hell's goin' on, Jack?' gasped Audrey, when she had recovered her breath.

'Someone's jest shot Phineas.'

'Is he . . . is he dead?'

'I dunno for sure, but I think so.'

'Oh, my God!'

'I guess we've been set up.'

'But why? An' . . . by whom?'

The Kentuckian didn't answer for some moments.

'It's gotta be Sam McCluskey an' his gang,' he said finally.

'But they're in jail in Kingman!'

'I don't think so.'

'Those fellers we overheard in the Buckin' Bronco said — '

'As I said, we was set up.'

'By them?'

'Yeah, by them. D'you remember, back in Bonnie Springs, the marshal told us that some li'l ol' white-haired, bespectacled feller in a black coat an' stovepipe hat rode in at first light? He didn't b'lieve that feller was connected with McCluskey an' his gang, but I reckon he was wrong.'

'Of course! That description exactly fits one of those two fellers we spoke to.'

'Which means that the gang *are* in

Flagstaff an' aimin' to raid the bank there.' Stone paused, then added quietly, 'I guess one of their number was detailed to trail us outa town with the intention of bushwhackin' us.'

'So, what now, Jack?'

'I'm gonna go git me that goddam bush-whacker an' then we head back to Flagstaff. Meantime, Audrey, you stay here an' keep your head down.'

'OK, but be careful.'

'Don't worry, I will be.'

Stone smiled grimly and began crawling along the dried-up water-course towards the nearest hillside. The arroyo wound its way round the base of the hill and, as soon as he was at its far side and out of sight of his would-be killer, the Kentuckian climbed out of the arroyo. Slowly, quietly, he scrambled up the hillside until he reached the summit.

Stone knew that the gunman would have to make a move sooner or later. He was right. The outlaw had to finish what he had begun. Quarter of an hour passed and then Stone saw the horseman ride down from the hills and onto the trail. McCluskey proceeded cautiously in the direction of the hollow, the Sharps rifle replaced in the saddleboot and his Remington revolver grasped in his right hand.

Stone's years as an Army scout stood him in good stead. He slipped down the hillside as silently as an Apache, gliding from rock to rock until he reached a tumble of boulders situated to one side of the trail and only a few yards from the entrance to the hollow in which Arizona Audrey remained hiding.

The Kentuckian drew his revolver and watched as the rider approached. Then, as the dark shape of man and horse drew level with the tumble of boulders, Stone suddenly stood up and stepped out onto the trail.

'Lookin' for me?' he enquired.

The outlaw started, then turned in the saddle, raised his gun and quickly took aim. But he was too late. Stone fired: once, twice, thrice.

All three bullets found their mark.

Two struck McCluskey in the chest, while the third drilled a hole in his cheekbone and exploded inside his skull, sending splinters of bone and fragments of brain blasting out of the back of his head. McCluskey was dead before he hit the ground, the force of the slugs having knocked him clean out of the saddle.

'OK, Audrey, you can come outa there now,' said Stone.

A rather dishevelled and thoroughly frightened Arizona Audrey climbed nervously out of the arroyo and then hurried across and threw herself into the Kentuckian's arms.

'Jeeze, Jack, that's McCluskey! Is . . . is he dead?' she whispered.

'Yup. Sam McCluskey ain't gonna bother us no more.'

'What . . . what about Phineas?'

'I'll go see.'

'I'll come with you.'

'OK. Only you'd best not look too close.'

Stone was right, for Phineas Yeats

presented a pretty awful sight. McCluskey's bullet had killed the Pinkerton man instantly, entering the back of his skull and exiting through the front. As a result, Yeats' face was a bloody mess. Also, his clothes were badly scorched where he had fallen upon, and more or less extinguished, the campfire.

'Oh, dear God!' exclaimed the blonde. 'What . . . what are we gonna do with him?'

'Take him back to Flagstaff, I guess,' replied Stone, adding grimly, 'I sure hope we can git there 'fore McCluskey's pardners carry out their bank raid.'

He carried the dead detective across to where his horse was tethered and laid him across the saddle. Then, fetching some cord from one of his saddle-bags, he tied him on securely. This done, Stone proceeded to do the same with the corpse of Sam McCluskey.

A few minutes later, he and Arizona Audrey were riding back along the trail in the direction of Flagstaff. Stone was leading the horse bearing Sam McCluskey, while Audrey was leading the one bearing Phineas Yeats. They rode at a gallop and in silence.

9

Slim Jim Linn played poker into the small hours of Sunday morning. Having to concentrate on the cards helped keep his mind off the planned bank raid. Afterwards, he retired to the room he had booked at the Alhambra Hotel and tossed and turned until dawn.

At half past eight that morning Slim Jim finally made up his mind. He had done reasonably well at the card-table. There was now no need for him to participate in J. C. Sharkey's nefarious project, for he was no longer broke. Therefore, he would do what he had been prevented from doing on the previous moming: slip quietly out of town and head east, where he figured he should be safe from pursuit. He would make for one of the big cities, New York or maybe Boston.

Unfortunately, once again he was

thwarted. When he descended the stairs into the lobby, he found J. C. Sharkey standing there, saying fond farewells to the voluptuous redhead with whom he had spent his two nights in Flagstaff.

'Ah, Slim Jim!' cried Sharkey. 'We shall walk together to Miguel's.' He handed the gambler a small canvas bag. 'All you need to blow that safe,' he explained in a low voice.

Slim Jim took hold of the bag and forced a smile.

'S . . . splendid!' he said, although what he really meant was, 'Goddammit to hell!'

They sat over breakfast in Miguel's for some minutes before the Delgado brothers joined them. Luis declined any food on behalf of himself and his brother, saying they had already eaten. The brothers did, however, partake of some coffee and, while they sipped it, Sharkey quickly reiterated his plan. Then, when he had finished, he asked, 'Is that quite clear?'

'*Sí*, J.C.' said Luis Delgado.

'OK. You got anythin' to add, Slim Jim?'

'Jest that carryin' this dynamite makes me kinda nervous.'

'So?'

'So, J.C., how's about if I go straight to the bank, while you go git that key off the bank manager? I'll wait outside the back door. Nobody ain't likely to see me there.'

'Guess not. Mebbe that's sensible.' Sharkey turned to the two Mexicans and snapped, 'Reckon it's time we paid Mr Casson that visit.'

The four men rose and left the restaurant. Each was carrying a pair of saddle-bags, ready to stuff with bank-notes. Sharkey led the way, closely followed by Slim Jim Linn, with the Delgado brothers bringing up the rear. They walked quickly through the deserted Main Street. The tented village had long since been dismantled, the horse dealers, roustabouts, wranglers, entertainers and other assorted visitors had gone and the townsfolk were indoors, either still enjoying breakfast or preparing themselves for church. In consequence, nobody spotted the trio as they made their way towards Silas Casson's large, redbrick house on the edge of town. Neither did they see Slim Jim as he left the others and walked slowly round to the rear of the bank. The gambler's instincts still told him to flee. But he did not. It was too late. He determined to play the cards that had been dealt to him.

J. C. Sharkey opened the small gate in the white-painted picket fence and headed up the short path to the bank manager's front door. He knocked three times and waited. The door opened to reveal a partially dressed Silas Casson. The bank manager wore neither collar, tie, vest nor jacket. Bright red suspenders held up his grey pin-striped trousers.

'Why, Mr . . . er . . . ? You called at the bank on Friday, I believe, and said . . . ' began Casson, upon recognizing his caller.

Sharkey cut him short. He pulled the pearl-handled British Tranter from his holster, rammed it hard into Casson's belly and snapped, 'Shuddup an' step inside!'

The bank manager didn't argue. The colour drained from his cheeks and there was fear in his eyes. He backed quickly into the house and, at Sharkey's prodding, continued on through a small hallway and into a large, spacious kitchen. Two young girls, one eleven and the other twelve, sat at the kitchen table finishing their breakfast, while their mother, a slender, blonde-haired woman in her mid-thirties, stood at the sink washing up. All three gasped at the sight of Silas Casson being forced into the kitchen at gunpoint. The appearance of J. C. Sharkey and his two confederates did nothing to reassure them.

'I want no hollerin' from you two,' Sharkey warned the two little girls. 'You start screamin' an' your daddy dies.' He turned to face the woman. 'The same applies to you,' he rasped.

'What . . . what do you want?' she gasped.

'Jest the key to open the bank's back door.'

'I can't give you that!' exclaimed Casson.

'You can an' you will.'

'But — '

'No buts, Mr Carson. You do as I tell you an' nobody gits hurt. On the other hand . . . '

The menace in Sharkey's voice and the icy look in his eye were enough to change the bank manager's mind. The outlaw did not have to complete his threat.

'OK! OK! I'll go fetch the key. It's in my bedroom,' said Carson.

'Go with him, Luis,' said Sharkey.

'*Sí*!'

The tall, lanky Mexican drew his Remington and followed Casson upstairs.

While the others awaited their return, Sharkey opened one of his saddle-bags and produced several lengths of cord and some strips of cotton cloth.

'Bind an' gag 'em, José,' he instructed the shorter, stockier of the two brothers.

'*Sí*.'

'You, ma'am, an' your gals, don't offer no resistance now an', like I said, nobody gits hurt.'

'We could slit their throats,' suggested José hopefully. 'It would be less trouble.'

'Bindin' an' gaggin' 'em ain't that much trouble. So, jest do as I say,' said Sharkey.

The Mexican made no further objection, but simply shrugged his shoulders and proceeded to do Sharkey's bidding.

He was still occupied with this task when Luis Delgado and the bank manager returned from their foray upstairs. Luis clutched a large key in one hand and his revolver in the other. He handed the key to Sharkey. The little old outlaw took it and smiled.

'See,' he said brightly. 'That was nice'n easy.'

'You . . . you won't git away with

this!' retorted Casson.

'Aw, but I reckon we will!' drawled Sharkey. He grinned at Luis Delgado and said, 'Bind an' gag him, will you, Luis?'

'*Sí*!'

'Thanks.'

Sharkey dropped the British Tranter back into its holster and waited patiently while the brothers completed their task. Both were thorough. There was no chance that Silas Casson, or any of his family, would slip either their bonds or their gags.

Sharkey removed the gold hunter from his vest pocket and studied it carefully. Then he returned it to the pocket and declared, 'We're 'bout on time, gents, so let's head straight for the bank.'

The bank was a ten-minute walk away. They did not approach it from Main Street, but from the rear. Upon reaching the bank, where they found Slim Jim anxiously waiting for them, Sharkey turned to the two Mexicans.

'OK, leave them saddle-bags with me an' Slim Jim, an' go git the hosses,' he commanded.

'*Sí*, J.C.'

'An' then wait for the bang.'

'*Sí*, J.C.'

'Right, now we'd best git inside as quick as we can,' he muttered.

Sharkey swiftly unlocked the door and hurried into the bank, carrying both his own and the brothers' saddle-bags. Slim Jim Linn followed with his saddle-bags and the small canvas bag containing the equipment needed to blow open the safe. The gambler handled the canvas bag very gingerly indeed.

They placed the saddle-bags on the floor on the customers' side of the bank counter, then retraced their steps. Sharkey opened the door of the manager's office and pointed at the huge steel contraption standing in the far corner.

'There's your safe, Slim Jim,' he said genially. 'Go to it!'

'How long have we got?' asked the safe-blower.

'If'n you're to blow it at precisely five past ten, you got ten minutes.'

'I . . . I'll do my best.'

J. C. Sharkey laughed.

'I guess it don't need to be that precise,' he admitted.

'No?'

'Nope. Jest so long as it blows while everybody in town's still in church.'

'Fine.'

But it was not fine. Slim Jim still could not, for the life of him, remember how many sticks of dynamite he had used to blow the one and only safe he had ever tackled. Before participating in Fats Bentley's bank raid, he had required a certain amount of Dutch courage. Consequently, unbeknown to Fats Bentley, he had blown open the safe while full of red-eye. It had, it seems, been a perfect job, but unfortunately, he had only the haziest of recollections of the occasion.

'While you fix up that there explosives

charge, I'll keep a lookout,' said Sharkey.

'OK, J.C.'

Slim Jim watched as the other lifted the flap, passed by the counter and crossed the floor of the bank, to stand peering out through one of the windows onto Main Street. Then, he cautiously opened the canvas bag and extracted in succession the six sticks of dynamite, the fulminate caps, the roll of sticky tape and the length of fuse. He stared anxiously at the huge steel safe. That, he figured, would take some blasting open! He decided, therefore, to go for broke and use all six sticks of dynamite. Handling them, while he fixed them to the door of the safe with the sticky tape, was not something Slim Jim did lightly. By the time they were securely attached, his hands were trembling, he was perspiring from every pore and his heart was beating like some demented steam-hammer.

Slim Jim paused for a few moments to regain his composure. He wiped his brow and forced himself to take deep breaths. Gradually, his heartbeats returned to normal. He smiled nervously and began to lay out the length of fuse. It stretched out through the manager's office, across the space behind the counter where the tellers worked, and into that part of the bank where the customers waited. He drew it round the counter to a point almost directly opposite the safe. Then he felt in his jacket pocket and withdrew a packet of lucifers.

'I'm ready, J.C.,' he called softly.

Sharkey again removed the gold hunter from his vest pocket and checked the time. He grinned.

'Well done, you're plumb on time. Light the fuse, Slim Jim.'

'OK, J.C.'

It took three attempts before the gambler succeeded in striking a light. Then, with a shaking hand, he finally lit the fuse. Immediately, the fuse began to burn. Slim Jim watched it burn its way across the floor and fizz off round the counter. As it vanished, he ducked down behind the counter where, seconds later, he was joined by J. C. Sharkey.

They crouched there in silence, waiting. The wait seemed interminable. The seconds ticked by, but still there was no explosion. Sharkey began to look worried. He glanced quizzically at the gambler.

'D'you think the fuse has burned itself out?' he enquired.

'I dunno,' said Slim Jim.

'Wa'al, you'd best find out.'

'But . . . but how?'

'Go an' look.'

'I don't think — '

'Go an' look.'

There was no denying the bank robber's command. J. C. Sharkey's glare and his tone told Slim Jim that much. Slowly, reluctantly, the gambler rose to his feet. As he did so, the burning fuse finally reached its target and the six sticks of dynamite ignited and exploded.

The explosion was enormous, far greater than was needed or intended. The massive steel door of the safe was blasted clean off its hinges and hurled across the manager's office. It sailed through the open doorway to crash into the counter, smashing that solid mahogany structure into matchwood. Sharkey survived only by throwing himself sideways in the nick of time. As for Slim Jim Linn, he was blown across the bank and out through the window. He landed with a thump on the sidewalk and was straightway buried beneath a pile of splintered glass, wooden planks and shattered roof-tiles.

Dazed and with his ears ringing, Sharkey staggered to his feet. He surveyed the scene surrounding him. Half the roof had been blown away, much of the front wall was in a state of collapse and the rest of it lay scattered across Main Street. The safe was minus its door, and its contents were fluttering out through the front of the bank like so much confetti. In time the banknotes could be retrieved, but Sharkey did not have time. He cursed loud and long, heaping obscenities on the head of the architect of the disaster, his luckless and incompetent safe-blower, Slim Jim Linn. He also swore to himself that, should he ever meet up with Fats Bentley, he would make him rue the day he had sung Slim Jim's praises.

The scene, which greeted him as he stepped out into Main Street, did nothing to improve Sharkey's temper. He reached the sidewalk just in time to witness the demise of the Delgado brothers.

Luis and José Delgado had been waiting with the four horses outside the Bucking Bronco saloon when the huge explosion occurred.

Its immensity had startled the Mexicans and frightened the horses. Consequently, crucial moments had passed before Luis and José could calm the animals, time which the two bandits could ill afford.

Sheriff John Baldwin and his deputies took it in turn to attend church on the Sabbath. Today it was Baldwin's turn to miss church and man the law office. At the sound of the explosion, he erupted out of the office like a cork out of a bottle of champagne. Straightway, he observed the Delgados struggling with the four horses in front of the Bucking Bronco.

Drawing his Colt Peacemaker and hurrying down the steps from the sidewalk to the street, the sheriff yelled, 'Stay where y'are an' stick your hands up!'

'I do not think so,' replied Luis Delgado.

The bandit sent one of the two horses he was holding trotting off in the direction of the bank and hastily pulled a Remington from beneath his poncho. He and the sheriff fired simultaneously. But the lawman had had time to take proper aim, whereas the outlaw did not. Therefore, Luis' shot went well wide of its mark while Baldwin's hit Luis between the eyes.

José had the drop on Baldwin and undoubtedly would have avenged his brother's death, but for the fact that

Larry Quince, the proprietor of the Bucking Bronco, was a confirmed atheist. Quince was one of the very few of Flagstaff's citizens *not* to be in church that morning. And the explosion had also brought him outside to see what was happening. He barged through the batwing doors, clutching his shotgun. The sight of José Delgado drawing a bead on the sheriff prompted him into immediate action. He took aim and squeezed the trigger of the scattergun. The two barrels blasted forth a wide-spreading diamond pattern of buckshot into the back of the Mexican. José screamed, dropped his revolver and fell face-downwards in the dust.

Sheriff John Baldwin dashed across Main Street, gun in hand. He ignored the fallen figure of Luis Delgado, who was clearly dead. As he approached José the Mexican tried to rise. His hand stretched towards the revolver he had dropped. But to no avail. Baldwin raised his Colt Peacemaker and emptied it into the bandit.

This was a mistake, since it allowed J. C. Sharkey to escape. The townsfolk, having rushed out of the church, were still some way off and, while Baldwin hurriedly reloaded the revolver, Sharkey was able to catch the horse which Luis Delgado had sent trotting in his direction.

The bank robber quickly swung into the saddle, dug his heels into the horse's flanks and galloped away from the fast-approaching crowd. And, although Baldwin did manage to loose off a couple of shots at his retreating back, Sharkey was by then just out of range.

Baldwin's three deputies were the first to arrive upon the scene. Baldwin told two of them to saddle up and get after the outlaw, while the third he ordered to guard the area round the front of the bank until the banknotes that littered the sidewalk could be retrieved, taken inside and counted.

Then, spotting Bob Garner among the crowd that had gathered, he said,

'Git yourself over here, Bob. You're the very man to gather up an' count these here banknotes.'

'Yessir,' said the young bank clerk, pushing his way to the front of the crowd.

'Where's Mr Casson, by the way?' enquired the sheriff.

'Dunno,' said Garner.

'He wasn't in church. Neither was Molly or the girls,' piped up Reuben Lloyd, the owner of the Alhambra Hotel, who, with his family, invariably occupied the same pew as the Cassons.

'No?' Baldwin looked worried. 'I'd best go check their house. See if they're there,' he said.

'Before you go, Sheriff, there's somethin' over here you oughta see,' said the deputy whom he had detailed to guard the bank.

'What's that, Roy?' demanded the sheriff.

'There's someone lyin' buried under all this rubble,' said Roy, pointing at the spot where part of the front wall had collapsed, together with a large portion of the roof. As he spoke, Slim Jim Linn, having only just recovered consciousness, crawled out from among the debris. He bore several cuts and bruises and was covered in dust.

'You're under arrest!' barked Baldwin.

Slim Jim slowly, groggily, rose to his feet, shaking his head. Although still dazed, he realized the perilous position in which he found himself. A spot of quick thinking was needed.

'What . . . what for?' he mumbled.

'For attempted bank robbery,' said Baldwin.

'Two of your pardners got theirselves shot an' one got away. But he's bein' pursued by two of my deppities. As for you, my friend, you ain't goin' nowhere. You are gonna spend the next few days in jail. Till we can git round to tryin' you. Then, I reckon you'll hang.'

'But I ain't part of no gang!'

'No?'

'No. Name's James Brown. I'm jest a

gamblin' man. Was playin' poker last night at the Alhambra an' figured I'd git me some fresh air this mornin'. I was walkin' past the bank, mindin' my own business, when the whole goddam place blew up an' collapsed about my ears. Hell, I could've been killed!'

'I don't believe a word — '

'He *was* playin' poker last night at the Alhambra,' interjected Reuben Lloyd.

'Yeah, wa'al, that don't prove nuthin',' said Baldwin. 'You're comin' with me, Mr Brown. We're gonna pay a call on the manager of this here bank. I hope for your sake I find him an' his family unharmed.'

The sheriff stepped up to Slim Jim, slipped his hand inside the gambler's jacket and withdrew the .30 calibre revolver, which he tossed on to the ground. Then, ramming his Colt Peacemaker into Slim Jim's ribs, he marched him off towards Silas Casson's house.

It was about this same time that J. C. Sharkey, upon rounding a bend in the trail, found himself face-to-face with Jack Stone and Arizona Audrey. As all three reined in their horses, the bank robber observed the two spare horses and their gruesome burdens.

'Wa'al, wa'al,' said Stone. 'Who do we have here?'

'It's the feller who sent us on a fool's errand to Kingman,' said Audrey.

'So it is.' The Kentuckian grinned. 'Would I be correct in guessin' that things ain't gone exactly to plan?' he asked.

'Yes, goddam you, Stone!' snarled Sharkey.

'You recognize me?'

'Saw you once in Dodge City, but I'd heard you'd retired.'

'I have. It's jest your bad luck I chanced to git involved in this, Mr . . . er . . . ?'

'Sharkey.'

The Kentuckian whistled softly.

'J. C. Sharkey?' he said.

'That's me.'

'You're somethin' of a legend out

here in the West.'

'As are you, Mr Stone.'

'Anyways, I'm takin' you in.'

'Aw, no, you ain't! Nobody takes in J. C. Sharkey.'

The little bank robber dropped his hand onto the pearl handle of his British Tranter. But he wasn't as fast as he used to be. While he was still quick enough to out-shoot the likes of Lanky Oates and his pals, he was nowhere near quick enough to match a gun-fighter of Jack Stone's calibre.

Before he could even clear leather, Stone's Frontier Model Colt was out and blazing. Two slugs hit Sharkey in quick succession. The first struck him in the chest, smashing through his ribcage. The second shattered the right-hand lense of his spectacles, demolished his eye-ball and exploded inside his brain. J. C. Sharkey had raided his last bank.

10

The arrival of Jack Stone and Arizona Audrey in Flagstaff, trailing three corpses, caused a minor sensation. Eventually, when the corpses of Phineas Yeats, Sam McCluskey and J. C. Sharkey had been moved by the mortician to the funeral parlour, Stone and the blonde adjourned, together with Sheriff John Baldwin, one of his deputies and Silas Casson, to the law office.

Explanations were given, pretty much the whole story of Sharkey's raid on the First National Bank was revealed and, at the conclusion of their talk, Silas Casson turned to Jack Stone and Arizona Audrey and said warmly, 'I wanta thank you folks on behalf of the bank. You sure saved it a whole heap of money.'

'I dunno 'bout that,' grinned Stone. 'I'd say it was the incompetence of

Sharkey's safe-blower that really foiled Sharkey.'

'Talkin' of which,' said Baldwin, 'we got the sonofabitch behind bars. I reckon he's gotta be the safe blower for, as far as I know, none of the others, includin' Sharkey, practised that partickler trade.'

'But the feller denies he was part of Sharkey's gang,' said Baldwin's deputy.

'He would, wouldn't he?' retorted Baldwin.

'Guess he would at that,' agreed Stone.

'Yeah, wa'al, we've already established there was five of 'em in the gang: Sharkey, McCluskey, them two Mexican killers an' one other. I maintain our prisoner is the fifth member. Go fetch him, Roy.'

'OK, Sheriff.'

The law office also acted as town jail. There were four cells situated at its rear, and it was from one of these that the deputy brought forth Slim Jim Linn. He looked thoroughly dejected and the unexpected sight of Arizona

Audrey did nothing to raise his spirits. His years as a professional gambler, however, helped him maintain an impassive visage. He straightened his shoulders and determined to bluff it out.

'I assume you are gonna release me, Sheriff?' he remarked.

'Nope.'

'But I am an innocent man! Like I said, I was jest walkin' past the bank when, all of a sudden — '

'Shuddup.' Baldwin glared at the gambler. 'Up till now nobody could definitely identify you as a member of Sharkey's gang, but Arizona Audrey can. Tell us, Arizona, is this lunkhead the feller who lured you outa Bonnie Springs an' abandoned you way out in the mountains?'

Audrey gazed long and hard at Slim Jim while the others waited expectantly. Finally, she spoke.

'No, this ain't the feller. I've never seen him before in my life.'

The sheriff gasped and stared incredulously at the blonde.

'Are you sure?' he rasped.

'Positive,' said Audrey.

'But . . . but, if he ain't the fifth member of Sharkey's gang, how in blue blazes did the bastard manage to escape?' exclaimed Baldwin.

'Mebbe he never came to Flagstaff. Mebbe he decided against takin' part in the raid an' split somewhere 'tween Bonnie Springs an' here,' suggested Stone.

'I s'pose,' said Baldwin dubiously.

'So, I can go?' enquired Slim Jim.

The sheriff glowered.

'Yup, Mr Brown, you can go,' he muttered, though with obvious reluctance.

'An' can I have my gun back?'

Baldwin had no alternative but to comply. He fetched the long-barrelled .30 calibre Colt and handed it to the gambler. Slim Jim returned it to the shoulder-rig, then raised his hat.

'Good day, folks,' he said, smiling, and left the law office.

Baldwin glanced at Arizona Audrey.

He remained unconvinced that Slim Jim was innocent. Yet the saloon-singer's testimony was irrefutable.

'Don't look so gloomy, Sheriff,' said Stone. 'The bank raid's been thwarted an' you got four dead bandits lyin' in the funeral parlour. That can't be bad.'

'No, I guess not.' Baldwin smiled wryly and asked, 'What are you plannin' to do now, Mr Stone?'

'I'm gonna send a wire to the Pinkerton Detective Agency in Chicago, to find out what's to be done with Phineas' body. If he has kith an' kin in Chicago, I expect it'll need to be shipped back there. If not, I aim to see that he gits a decent funeral here in Flagstaff.'

'Either way, the bank will pay all expenses,' declared Silas Casson.

'Thank you,' said Stone.

Thereupon, taking their leave of the sheriff and the bank manager, the Kentuckian and Arizona Audrey stepped outside into Main Street.

'Will you stop for Phineas' funeral

if'n it takes place here?' enquired Stone.

'Of course,' said Audrey. 'Afterwards, Jack, where are you headed?'

'South, though, naturally, I'll escort you back to Bonnie Springs first.'

'That won't be necessary.' Audrey gently patted her bottom. 'I ain't ridin' no more hosses. I reckon I'll take the stage.'

'Them stagecoaches ain't none too comfortable either,' grinned Stone.

'That's why I aim to buy me another cushion. I oughta make it with two cushions under me.'

'OK,' said Stone. 'Let's go send that telegraph an' git you that cushion. Then, I figure we'll mosey on back to the bar-room at the Alhambra for a few drinks, an' later . . .'

Arizona Audrey chuckled seductively. 'Sounds good to me, Jack,' she said.

They headed for the stage line depot, wherein was situated the telegraph office. Stone composed and sent his telegraph message and, immediately afterwards, they repaired to the dry goods store, where Audrey purchased another red satin cushion. It was as they approached the Alhambra that they spotted an elegant, black-clad figure unhitching his horse from the rail in front of the hotel. He swung up into the saddle and then, turning the horse's head, set off down Main Street. A smile of recognition creased his face upon spotting Stone and the girl.

'Howdy, folks,' he said, raising his hat.

'You leavin' town, Mr Brown?' enquired the Kentuckian.

'Yeah, guess I'll try my luck elsewhere,' said Slim Jim.

'Probably a wise move,' commented Audrey.

'Yes, ma'am,' said Slim Jim and, raising his hat a second time, he wished her and the Kentuckian good day.

'Good day, Mr Brown.'

They watched the gambler trot off down Main Street and then turned again towards the hotel.

As they clattered up the steps on to

the stoop, Stone glanced at his pretty companion and drawled, 'Despite what you said back at the law office, that *was* the feller who called hisself Jerome Muggeridge an' tricked you into drivin' out into the mountains with him wasn't it, Audrey?'

'Er . . . why . . . why should you think that, Jack?' she stammered.

'Don't worry. I ain't gonna go after him an' I ain't gonna tell the sheriff neither.'

'Wa'al, I dunno. I . . . '

'Aw, come on! Tell me, Audrey.'

Arizona Audrey smiled and shrugged her shoulders.

'OK,' she said. 'I confess. He was the feller. I lied 'cause I figured I owed him. He could've shot me like McCluskey told him to.'

'He could.'

'Anyways, him an' me, we're quits now.'

'Yup. I reckon you are,' said Stone.

Other titles in the Linford Western Library:

A TOWN CALLED TROUBLESOME

John Dyson

Matt Matthews had carved his ranch out of the wild Wyoming frontier. But he had his troubles. The big blow of '86 was catastrophic, with dead beeves littering the plains, and the oncoming winter presaged worse. On top of this, a gang of desperadoes had moved into the Snake River valley, killing, raping and rustling. All Matt can do is to take on the killers single-handed. But will he escape the hail of lead?

THE WIND WAGON

Troy Howard

Sheriff Al Corning was as tough as they came and with his four seasoned deputies he kept the peace in Laramie — at least until the squatters came. To fend off starvation, the settlers took some cattle off the cowmen, including Jonas Lefler. A hard, unforgiving man, Lefler retaliated with lynchings. Things got worse when one of the squatters revealed he was a former Texas lawman — and no mean shooter. Could Sheriff Corning prevent further bloodshed?

CABEL

Paul K. McAfee

Josh Cabel returned home from the Civil War to find his family all murdered by rioting members of Quantrill's band. The hunt for the killers led Josh to Colorado City where, after months of searching, he finally settled down to work on a ranch nearby. He saved the life of an Indian, who led him to a cache of weapons waiting for Sitting Bull's attack on the Whites. His involvement threw Cabel into grave danger. When the final confrontation came, who had the fastest — and deadlier — draw?